Creatures
at Christmas

Creatures
at Christmas

**Six Stories with Bite
and a special
Creatures song**

Louise Cooper

Scholastic Children's Books
Commonwealth House, 1–19 New Oxford Street,
London WC1A 1NU, UK
London ~ New York ~ Toronto ~ Sydney ~ Auckland
Mexico City ~ New Delhi ~ Hong Kong

First published by Scholastic Ltd, 1999

ISBN 0 439 01410 7

All rights reserved
Typeset by Falcon Oast Graphic Art
Printed by Cox & Wyman Ltd, Reading, Berks

2 4 6 8 10 9 7 5 3 1

Contents

Page

This poem is about my own cat, Spike. He's much too friendly and affectionate to be a *Creature*, and this is how he gives me some much-needed relief from scarier beasts!

Spike's Day

Pouncey round the sofa,
Pouncey round the door;
He has a game of Pouncey
And then he wants some more.
Pouncey on my fingers,
Pouncey on my feet,
Pouncey on his food dish,
For now it's time to eat.

Chasey in the kitchen,
Chasey through the house,
Chasey round the bedroom
After his toy mouse.
Chasey down the garden,
Chasey in the shed,
Chasey to his basket
And then it's time for bed.

Sprawly on the duvet,
Sprawly on the chair,
Sprawly on a velvet jacket,
Shedding lots of hair.
Sprawly on my keyboard,
Making it go *bleep*,
Then sprawly-purry round my neck –
It's time to go to sleep!

How Much is That Doggy in the Window?

22 December

I *knew* they'd choose me. Soon as they came into the kennels, I thought: They're all right; they'll do. So I put the old "influence" on 'em. I'm good at that. *Very* good. And I was on my best behaviour, too, did the whole act: big brown eyes, happy grin, wriggle-wriggle, wag my tail till it nearly fell off. Worked a treat. The younger woman went "Aaah!" and came over all gooey, and the older one said, "We'll take him. Go on then, Brian, get your chequebook out."

He didn't look too pleased, but he paid up. I didn't know pedigree puppies cost *that* much! Mind you, he's not exactly getting an ordinary pedigree puppy, is he? Not at all. But then, I'm the only one who knows that little secret. The other pups in the litter are too young to be bothered about me, and as for their mum ... well, she's so dimwitted and pampered, she didn't even notice when an extra, furry, snuffling bundle sneaked into her basket on the night the pups were born and added himself to the total. *Heh, heh.*

So now I'm going home. Sounds great, doesn't it? *Home.* Little old me. (*Heh, heh...*) Apparently, I'm a Christmas present for their little boy, Joe. They're not being irresponsible, mind: they know that a dog's for life and not just for Christmas ('scuse me pinching that phrase) and they'll look after me properly. I heard them say they'll have to hide me in the spare bedroom till Christmas morning, so I'm a proper surprise, but that's OK. Probably be fun, in fact. A lot of fun.

I'm looking forward to this.

24 December

I don't *believe* it. I really don't.

No, it's not the new home; that's fine. Food's decent, I've got my own bed, all nice and cosy, toys to play with and all that. No. It's the *name.*

Oh sure, I knew they'd give me a name. I mean, they don't know my *real* name, and I wouldn't tell them it even if I could. They'd get the wrong idea, wouldn't they? Might worry them. But...

I don't want to tell you. It makes my blood boil even to think about it. But if you're going to understand, well, I suppose... Oh, all right then. Deep breath, gritted teeth...

Floppy. Those clod-hopping, two-legged *idiots* have called me *Floppy*! Why? Because I've got big paws and floppy ears and a waggly tail, that's why! Or to put it another way, because they're so unbelievably cretinous that they can't see the truth when it's staring them in the face! That woman – Mum – said it sounded *cute*. "Floppy Puppy," she calls me. *Grrrrr!* All right, so puppies *are* floppy, but what sort of excuse is that? Do they think I'm going to stay cute for ever? Don't they realize that I'm going to GROW UP???

I'm not putting up with this. Not for long. They'd better change their minds and come up with something more suitable, *or else*.

OK, OK; I won't do anything yet. Maybe Joe – the kid whose present I am – will stick up for me and tell them what they can do with flippin' Floppy. We'll see. I'm patient. I can wait till tomorrow.

25 December
And a happy perishing Christmas to you, too!

"Here he is, Joe, here's your present. A dear little doggie, all your very own. *Aaah!*"

I'll give them "*aaah*". Stand up for me? Joe? Stand *on* me, more likely, while poking a finger in my ear and pulling my tail at the same time. Joe, you see, is three years old. Three. Just the age of kid that dogs can't stand. I'm not his dog at all, of course; they just pretend to him, because they were too mean to buy him a Super Exterminator Bam-Bam Ballistic Missile Gun or whatever it was he really wanted for Christmas. He's *pleased* with me. Oh, yeah; he's so pleased that he tried to hug me and nearly broke ten of my ribs in the process. I didn't bite him; I thought: hang on a bit, if he sorts out the name business then I'll let him off this once. But did he sort it out? *Ha!*

"He's called Floppy," they gooed at him. "Isn't that sweet?" And what does Joe do? He grins like a dead haddock and he says, "Flobby!" He can't even pronounce Floppy; he says *Flobby* instead! And now it's STUCK, and I'm Flobby to this whole houseful of idiots!

THIS IS INTOLERABLE! AND I'M GOING TO DO SOMETHING ABOUT IT!

OK, OK, I'm calming down. You don't get anywhere by throwing wobblers and going over the top; not at this stage, anyway. What I need to do is think. Make some plans. Get a strategy worked out. Better to bide my time and make sure I do this *properly*.

Hmm... The Christmas dinner smells good, I'll give 'em that. And they've promised me some. Maybe I'll eat myself sick, then puke up on that expensive rug by the hearth. Well, it's a start, isn't it?

Though if they think it's going to stop there, all I can say is: they're going to learn just how very wrong they are.

Oh, yes. Very, very wrong *indeed*...

26 December

Right. The first part of any strategy is, get to know your enemy. Basically, there's six of them, if you don't count the budgie (and there's no point, because that feathered green rat in disguise isn't going to be around much longer). There's Mum, Dad, Nan, Joe, Joe's big sister, Pauline, and his bigger brother, Mark. That's the lot. So, who's going to be first? I can't quite make up my mind between Joe and Nan at the moment. Probably Nan, because Joe... Well, you've got to make some allowances for little kids, haven't you?

Hang on: I'd forgotten the budgie. Billy-Boy the Blasted Budgie. *Squawk, squawk,* "Who's a pretty boy, then?" and banging his beak on that stupid little bell every ten seconds. Drives me *nuts*. But I might have put up with it if the dumb bird hadn't learned one new word.

You guessed it. Flobby. It took Joe about point-three of a second to teach it to Billy-Boy, so now it's "Flobby-Flobby-*Flobby*" morning, noon and night. That detestable bird *knows* it means me, and he knows how much it winds me up. He thinks he's all safe and sound, swinging away up there in his cage. He thinks I'm too small to climb up there and get him.

Isn't *he* in for a surprise!

And it'll be good practice.

Hmm … talking of practice, I suppose I ought to work out a bit before I get down to the real stuff. After all, I haven't done this for a while; last time was … what, six months ago? Yeah, must have been. At the rescue shelter, when I … well, never mind what I did. Let's just say that I lay low for a while after that, until I got the chance to sneak in with that dimwit pedigree pooch and her pups.

Right: there's no one around, they're all out or watching telly, so…

Deep breath. Eyes shut. Concentrate. *Flobby*, indeed! Keep thinking *Flobby*. Ah, that's it. I can feel myself getting riled. Getting really *angry*. Good, good. Here we go, then. Breathe in, and –

HAARRRRRGGGHHH! ARARRR! GNN-NNAAAAA!

Hey, I can still do it! Whooo... Brilliant. I haven't lost my touch! Wonder if they heard anything? Shouldn't think so; the telly's blaring too loudly. Right, then, I'm all set. Just you wait, Billy-Boy Budgie. Just you wait till they've all gone to bed tonight...

27 December
Got him! And I enjoyed *every moment* of it.

That idea about the neighbour's cat was a stroke of genius, if I say so myself. Just push the window open a bit, leave the cage door open and a few feathers on the floor, and in the morning it's Boo-hoo, poor little Billy-Boy, horrid old Tibbles, he must have got in and ... etc., etc.

The look on that bird's face when he saw me was worth all the effort it took to do it. Not that birds really have expressions, but you know what I mean. Scared, or wot? Well, if you'd seen what he saw: dear little, dinky little Flobby, suddenly turning into...

Ahem. Enough said. I don't think much of the taste of budgie. A bit fishy. And too many bones and feathers. Nothing like as good as turkey. They gave me some extra turkey this morning, because they said Tibbles must have frightened me. After all, I'm only a little floppy puppy, aren't I? *Aaah*.

The only person who did look at me a bit suspiciously was Nan. So I've decided – she'll be next. I'll just give it another day or two, to let things settle down after Billy-Boy. RIP, little birdie.

Heh, heh, heh…

3 January
They've all just come back from visiting Nan in hospital. From what they're saying, it sounds like she's going to be in there for a while. Well, got to give her leg time to mend, hasn't she? And all those bruises… Then when she does come out, she says she won't come back here. Never, ever. That's what all this fuss is about, because she won't tell them why. They're so agitated, they've forgotten to give me my dinner. I'll give 'em a bit longer to remember me, then I'll go and look cute at them and do the whine-whimper bit. Or bite someone.

No, no; mustn't give in to temptation! Getting rid of Nan was much more fun than dealing with Billy-Boy. I didn't even have to chase her, let alone anything more drastic. All on her own in the house, she was. So when she goes upstairs to the loo, I follow on tippy-toes and hide in the airing cupboard on the landing, right near the top of the staircase. Back comes Nan. Deep breath, *concentrate*, and –

HAARRRRRGGGHHH!

Well, if you'd seen what she saw then, you'd have screamed and jumped backwards, too, wouldn't you? It's a long way from the top to the bottom of those stairs, and she did it in about three seconds flat, head over heels. When the others came in she was out cold on the hall floor, with me sitting beside her like a faithful, bewildered doggy. Did Mum scream! She sounded like a banshee; I didn't think she had it in her.

Nan'll get better soon enough. Pity, really; I never liked her much. But at least she won't be setting foot in this house again. Not after what happened. And they'll *never* get the truth out of her, because if she did tell them, they'd think she was a loony. So she's going to live as far away from here as she can get. Inverness, I think they said. I reckon Dad's secretly pleased. He didn't like her much, either.

Ah, here comes my dinner at last. Mum's doing it. She's all tearful – hey, be careful! I don't want salt water dripping in my food. What is it? Oh. Peppy-Pup and Waggo Biscuits again.

Boring. She's mumbling at me as she puts the bowls down: "Dear little Flobby, poor doggy, he must have been so traumatized. Isn't he brave and faithful…" All together, now: "*Aaah…*"

Shows how much *she* knows!

Now Nan's gone, I suppose the rest of them aren't too bad, really. Even Joe. Like I said the other day, you have to make allowances, and I've got a very forgiving nature. Maybe from now on I'll tolerate them and only play the occasional little joke, just to keep in practice.

So long as they behave themselves.

8 January

I take that back. *All* of it. *Grrr!*

This time, it's Dad who's got me riled. You know what? He resents me. And it's all down to money.

Of course I'm growing up, aren't I? Dinky puppies turn into un-dinky dogs, and I'm being very careful to make sure I grow at the same rate as if I really was what they think I am. Well … maybe I've sped it up a *bit*. I mean, it's boring not being big enough to get on the sofa without someone helping me. And as I grow up, I need more food. Lots more food. Which costs money. And Dad, I've discovered, is a skinflint.

I first heard him grumbling to Mum a couple

of days ago about how much I'm costing him. He said it was all Nan's fault. He said he'd never have bought a blasted expensive blasted dog if Nan and Mum hadn't nagged him into it, and do they think he's made of money?

Mum got all aggressive at that, and said he was miserable and stingy, "And it's a different story when it comes to splashing out on your stupid gadgets, isn't it?"

So Dad said, "Oh, right, *gadgets*. What about Joe's kiddy-computer, then? As if that didn't cost enough as a Christmas present without buying him a stupid overpriced dog as well!"

They banged on at each other for about half an hour, then Mum went off to sulk. As soon as she was out of the room, Dad gave me a sly look. Then he kicked me. Not hard – it was really just a sort of nudge with his foot. But I knew what he was thinking. I didn't whine or whimper. There was no one else around, so I wouldn't have got any sympathy. But if he thinks I'm not going to get my own back, he's got another think coming. He always leaves his trainers by the back door. Tonight, I'll eat them. Just as a gentle warning. If he doesn't get the message … well, I'll have to take sterner measures.

Much sterner.

9 January

Dad's next. I'm going to get him.

Yeah, I ate the trainers, and pretty disgusting they were too. He came downstairs, saw the chewed remains, and saw me, head down, eyes glaring, staring at him. He got the message all right: "That's what you get for messing with me, Sunshine!" And you know what he did? He took off one of his slippers, and he *whacked* me with it! Called me Bad Dog, and Stupid Brute, and all kinds of other things I wouldn't dream of repeating in polite company. Then he picked me up, shoved me out in the garden and wouldn't let me back in again for an hour.

That is *it*. If Dad hasn't got the intelligence to know what's good for him, then he'll have to learn the hard way. OK, mate. You just wait till Saturday...

13 January

Two-nil! And it was *great*!

Mum's dead right about Dad and his gadgets – he's completely loopy about them. He's got a workshop at one end of the garage, and it's full of *every* sort of gizmo you can imagine. I'm not allowed in there, of course. When the door's shut, there aren't any gaps big enough for even a li'l ol' puppy to squeeze through.

But I'm not any li'l ol' puppy, am I?

Saturday morning, and off Dad goes as usual to the workshop. He never actually does anything useful. Everything he makes falls to bits, and if he tries to repair something, it ends up worse than when he started. Drives Mum nuts. Anyway, this Saturday he decided he was going to "tidy up" in there. About time, too. The place is a complete tip. He's got these rickety slot-together metal shelves all over the place, and they're piled with every sort of junk you can imagine, and quite a few you can't. Then he's rigged up these other storage boxes, which hang under the roof and are carried up and down by this home-made pulley system. It looks extremely precarious, but he swears it's as safe as houses.

I was watching when he got started. He didn't know I was there. Dad's idea of "tidying" was to haul those pulley-boxes down, stuff them with everything he couldn't find a better place for, then haul them up to the roof again. After about an hour he got bored with that, and decided to play with his toys instead.

Dad's latest project is to strip the paint off a hideous "antique" table that he bought in a junk shop because it was cheap. He thinks he can "restore" it, then sell it again for loads of money.

That'll be the day! So he fetched his super-duper guzzle-box of a blowtorch thing and got down to work.

I watched for a bit as the blowtorch roared and sizzled. He was getting the paint off OK, but the fumes were making him go woozy, and his hand started to wobble so much that he was burning whopping great gouges in the table. By the time he'd finished, the thing was going to look more prehistoric than antique. So I decided to put him out of his misery. Whoops, watch out, Dad! Woozy-poozy – you're waving that blowtorch around so much, you nearly scorched the pulley rope just now!

Heh, heh, heh.

Deep breath. Concentrate. He had his back to me and he was muttering, so in case he didn't hear, I thought I'd better make it good and loud. One – two – three –

ARARRR! GNNNNAAAAA!

Dad spun round as though someone had kicked him in the backside. In one split second he saw me, his eyes popped, his mouth opened, and –

"WAAAAAA!"

Over he went, crashing into his "priceless antique" and pulling it over on top of himself. The blowtorch went flying and landed exactly where I'd planned it to. Right beside the pulley rope. Still roaring. Still burning.

Dad was waving his arms and yelling, "*Waaa, no, help, get off, get away, help, aarrgh!*" I wasn't even doing anything. I just stood there, towering over him. Well, maybe I was grinning a bit. That sort of demonic grin that I'm good at. You know: whirling red eyes, gaping jaws, fangs dripping venom, the usual stuff. And I might have raised my front legs, with the sabre claws on them, in a sort of looming, menacing way. I only had a few seconds before people came running from the house. But that was all I needed. Because at that moment, the blowtorch burned through the pulley rope. There was an ominous creak overhead, then...

CRAAAAAASH!!!

The storage boxes under the roof came plummeting down like an avalanche. As they fell, they hit the rickety metal shelves. Wobble, sway – whooooops – *KA-BANG, CLATTER-CLATTER-CLATTER, SMAAAAASH!*

Luckily for Dad, the table protected him from the worst of it. Half a tonne of junk raining down didn't do the table a lot of good, though. Demolished it, in fact.

As for the car...

Well, of course, when Mum came charging to

the rescue I wasn't there, was I? Not in the shape Dad had seen, anyway. Dear little, dinky little Flobby was hidden under the work-bench, with a grand view of the whole entertainment. Which went something like this:

Mum: "What happened, what happened?"

Dad: "Waaaaaa! I saw it! It was horrible!"

Mum: "What are you on about? Oh my God, look at this wreckage! You idiotic (*something*), what have you *done*?"

Dad: "But it was there! A hideous monster, a demon, a—"

Mum: "Oh, shut up! It's those fumes, isn't it? Phoo, I can smell them! You've done it again – you've made yourself go funny in the head with that paint-stripping!"

Joe's big brother, Mark, appeared at that point. Mark's quite sensible. He saw the blowtorch still burning and turned it off. Then he stared round the workshop. He stared at the car. He looked at Mum. Then he looked at Dad.

"Wow!" he said.

Heh, heh. They took Dad to Casualty, but it was only shock. He's still going on and on about the "monster" that attacked him. Naturally, no one believes a word. They all think it was a hallucination, caused by the fumes from the burned-off paint. I hear he got a lecture from the

18

Casualty doctor about working in confined spaces that aren't properly ventilated.

As for the car ... oh, dearie me. Apparently it wasn't insured for that sort of accident, so the insurance company are refusing to pay up. Oh, and later that day the workshop roof fell down, too. Something about the boxes putting too much strain on it. Mum went ballistic. Dad'll be lucky if she ever speaks to him again.

I reckon he's learned his lesson, though. He's not *completely* sure that the terrifying thing he saw was me. But when I did it, I was careful to make what I changed into sort of recognizable, so Dad's got a horrible inkling of the truth. He hasn't even thought about kicking or smacking me since. And he never grumbles, now, about how much I cost to feed.

Ahh. Life's definitely looking up. From now on, I think things are going to be nice and peaceful round here.

25 January
Me and my big mouth. Nice and peaceful? *Ha!*

It isn't that I hate *all* little kids. Some of them can be OK, fun to play with. But Joe... If he isn't the brat from hell, I don't know what is.

I've *tried* to be nice to him. So far, I've only bitten him three times when he pulled my tail, and they were only nips really. But did it stop him? No, it did not!

After virtually ignoring me for weeks, he's taken a fancy to me all of a sudden. I think it's because his new kiddy-computer's packed up and he's bored. So now, whenever he sees me, it's "Flobby-Flobby-Flobby!" and he comes charging at me like a tank, grabbing for any bit he can get hold of. Tail, legs, ears, it's all the same to him.

And what does Mum do when she sees her precious little angel pulling the dog to pieces? "Now, Joe," she coos, "be kind to poor Flobby! No, darling, don't try to unscrew his head; doggies' heads aren't supposed to come off. Play with him nicely. That's better," as the little thug starts rolling on me instead. "Look, Pauline, Mark – Joe's playing with the puppy. Isn't that lovely?" All together, now: *Aaah!*

And Joe goes his own sweet way. You'd think I was some indestructible cartoon character from his computer games; you know, turn me inside-out and I'll just come up smiling. Joe probably thinks that, too. He's too young, and too dumb, to know the difference between fantasy and reality.

Well, he'll just have to be shown, won't he?

That, though, is going to be a bit of a tricky

one to handle. Unfortunately, the third time I bit Joe, Mum saw me do it. Big mistake on my part. I got smacked on the nose with a rolled-up magazine and shut in the kitchen with no food for half an hour. Now, I've heard her talking to Pauline and Mark about *training*. No *way*. Mum's going to have to be next on my list, I can see that.

But only when I've dealt with Joe.

I've thought very hard about this, and I've come to the conclusion that there's only one way to do it without risking being caught by anyone else. It's going to have to be dead-of-night stuff, in the brat's bedroom. And if the message is going to get through to what passes for Joe's brain, there's no point being subtle. Forget the half-measures I used with Nan and Dad; this will have to be an all-out terror job. The real thing. Very real. Very, *very* real.

I'd better start building my strength up. Wouldn't do to run out of steam half-way through the transformation. So I'll stop my diary for a little while.

When I come back to it, I should have one heck of a story to tell.

Heh, heh, heh.

4 February
This is very, very painful for me. I truly never

21

thought that anything like this could ever happen. If I'd known – if I'd even *imagined* – then I would have behaved very differently. But now it's done, and it's far too late to change anything.

I don't want to talk about this. Even now it still makes me shiver when I remember it. But I can't escape from the truth. I've *got* to tell you.

All right, then. Here goes...

I spent more than a week getting ready for my confrontation with Joe. It was hard work, even harder than that time (while I was disguised as a Yorkshire terrier) when that nice young couple thought I was lost and took me home, and...

Ahem. Never mind; that was a very long time ago. Joe. Yes. As I said, it took more than a week to prepare myself. But at last I was ready, and what I had in mind was going to be the performance of a lifetime.

Mum and Dad had been out to see friends, leaving Pauline and Mark to babysit. Dad was a bit tipsy when they came home, and Mum got cross because she'd had to drive and so she couldn't have any wine. (She was speaking to him again, by the way. But she isn't again now.) There was another family row, just a small one, and they all went to bed feeling grumpy. Joe, of course, was already asleep. Perfect.

I crept upstairs very quietly. Puppies can be quiet when they want to. Past Pauline's room, then Mum and Dad's, then Mark's. And last of all, there was Joe's. The door was shut, but that was no problem. I just concentrated, changed into something a *teeny* bit more like my real self, and re-materialized on the other side. I can see perfectly in the dark. And there he was, Mum's little angel, sound asleep. He's got Disney characters all over his room: on the wallpaper, the curtains, the pillowcase, the duvet cover. Well, I thought, he's going to meet a new character tonight. And Disney's got nothing to do with it!

Heh, heh, heh.

I looked at his bust kiddy-computer. Joe had been getting quite good at playing the games, till the thing packed up. His favourites were the gruesome ones, full of monsters that you had to zap before they took over the world, or whatever. Joe always got them.

But not this time, Joey-boy, I told myself. This time, the monster's going to get *you!*

The best place to do it, I decided, was not at the end of the bed but at the side, so that the moment he opened his eyes, he'd be face to face with me. No towering and looming, either – not to start with, anyway. Much more effective if I was on a level with him. The rest could come afterwards, just so he wouldn't be left in any doubt as to what he was up against.

So I squatted down on the bedside mat and started my breathing exercises. (For something as major as this, breathing exercises are a good idea.) Right, then. Was I ready? Feeling fierce enough? Feeling *demonic* enough? You bet I was! This was going to be *fun*.

Deep breath. Concentrate. And...

"*Joe-y.*" (Lovable little voice. I'm good at that.) "*Joe-y. Wake up, Joe-y. Look who's come to play with you.*"

Yeah, kid, you just look. Ever seen anything like me before? Ever seen, in your worst nightmares, something that slowly turns from a dear little puppy-dog into a hulking, hunched, hairy horror, ten times bigger than you, with *grrreat* long front legs tipped with curving, deadly claws? Ever seen a face like this, all grinning and leering, with dripping fangs and whirling red eyes as big as dinner-plates? Ever heard a *snnnnaaaaarl* like mine?

"*Joe-y,*" I cooed again. The little brat hadn't even woken up yet. I wanted to shake him awake. But that would have spoiled some of the fun. "*Coo-ee, Joe-y! Wake-y, wake-y!*" (Hey, poetry!)

Aha! He stirred at last. A little fist clenched and he said, dreamily, "Bam-bam!" Playing computer games in his sleep. Typical.

"*Coo-ee, Joe-y!*" Come on, you little wretch, wake UP, will you?

Suddenly, he did. His eyes opened. And there I was, my face half a metre from his nose. It was – it had to be – the most horrific, terrifying, appalling thing that kid had ever seen in his LIFE!

And do you know what happened? Do you know? Can you guess? Can you *believe* it?

He – he –

Laughed!

That small, squirty, moronic runt of a little brat *laughed* at me!

HAARRRRRGGGHHH!

I reared up, swelling in size till my head banged on the ceiling. *ARARRR!* I went. *GNNNNAAAAA!* I shrieked. I made my face more hideous than ever. I sprouted horns. I grew four more front legs and waved them wildly at him. My tongue shot out two metres, dripping saliva everywhere.

NNNRRROOOOORGHHH! THRAAAAA! GLOBBER-GLOBBER, ARARRR, ARARRR, ARROOOOO!

I put everything I'd got into it. *Everything*. It

half-killed me! And that brat just bounced up and down on his bed, clapping his hands and chortling with delight!

"Bam!" he yelled. "Bam-bam-zap-BOOM, you're dead, I got you! Silly old monster!"

There was a commotion out on the landing. Voices, thudding feet – "What the hell was that?" "What's going on?" "Joe! JOE!"

Well, there was only one thing I could do, wasn't there?

I ran for it. Shamed as I am to admit it, I turned back into Flobby and I *bolted*. As the door opened I skidded between Dad's feet, away along the landing and down the stairs. I didn't stop till I reached the kitchen, where I slid to a halt on the back doormat, panting and gasping.

And totally, absolutely *mortified*.

Well, that's the whole ugly story of what happened to me. They're all still upstairs. I'm still sitting on the doormat. And I feel so humiliated I could curl up and die. *Me*, the deadly demon dog, outwitted by a horrible little three-year-old! To be *laughed* at, to be called a "silly old monster" … the *shame* of it! It's the worst thing that's ever happened in my entire life!

Well, I'm not staying here, that's for sure. I used up almost all my demon-energy with that performance. I've just about got enough left to dematerialize through the back door, but after that I'll be stuck with being Flobby Puppy for a bit. Can't be helped. I'm leaving, right *now*, before they come down and make things worse by being all gooey and pitying over me. Poor little Flobby, was he scared, then? Yeah, you bet poor little Flobby was scared! Scared to think that a mere *human*, and an extremely small one at that, could stand up to a fiendish creature that's caused havoc in more houses than he's ever had hot dinners, and *win*!

So that's it: I'm off, and I'll *never* show my face round here again. In fact, I've had enough of human beings altogether. As soon as I get my demon-strength back again, I'm going home. *My* home. For good. I don't care if all the other ghoulies and ghosties and long-leggedy beasties take the mickey and call me a wimp. It's all right for them; they get the easy jobs, like going "bump" in the night. They haven't *suffered* like I have!

So bye, bye, horrible human world. Don't think I'll *ever* come back, because I won't. You've seen the last of *this* dear, cute little puppy, with his floppy ears and his big brown eyes.

There's just one consolation. Never, ever

again will I have to listen to one particular thing. The thing they always used to say to me. Before they knew better. Before *I* knew better.

You know what that thing is. So, for the last time... All together now: *Aaah!*

Gobble, Gobble

OK, so a lot of the other kids at school called him fat. Olly didn't care. To start with, he was big enough to look after himself. Second, he had his own friends. And third, he didn't care a hoot anyway. Because Olly just *loved* food.

Which meant that, when Christmas came around, he was in his element. And this year in particular, Christmas promised to be absolute bliss.

It started when Mum announced that not only Gran and Grandad but Aunt Liz as well were coming to stay. Olly's ears pricked up at once. Gran knew all about him and what he liked – every time he saw her she gave him either sweets or some money for sweets; and Aunt Liz was his favourite aunt because she was plump and cheerful, and always had tonnes of food at her house, and (unlike Mum) never told him that four spoonfuls of cream on his pudding was more than enough and six just plain greedy. There'd be extra presents this year, he thought, and with any luck most of them would be edible.

Three evenings before Christmas, Olly and his parents and his twin kid sisters got together, as they always did, to decorate the tree. Sal and Sara had been getting more and more excited about it all day. They couldn't wait to lug the decorations box downstairs and start gloating over the baubles and tinsel and assorted bits and pieces, and they kept running to Olly to show him some special favourite. Olly went along with it. He could afford to be patient, because Mum had come back from the supermarket earlier, and he'd sneaked a look through the carrier bags before she unpacked them. He'd *seen* what was in there: nuts, satsumas, two gigantic tins of biscuits – one sweet, the other savoury – several fancy boxes of sweets – presents, no doubt, for Gran and Aunt Liz. And lots of new tree decorations.

Chocolate ones.

He'd only eaten three. He just couldn't resist. Mum had bought so many that she wouldn't miss them – he was probably doing her a favour, as there'd never be room for all that lot on the tree. And ... well, he'd had a couple of satsumas. And some walnuts. Olly loved walnuts. He thought about the boxes of sweets, but decided, reluctantly, that Mum *would* notice that, so he left them alone. It was a bit of an effort, but they'd get shared out on Christmas Day, anyway. Oh, yes; he only had to be patient for a while.

At teatime, Olly ate his usual size meal: four beefburgers with oven chips, relish, ketchup, piccalilli, baked beans and quarter of a loaf of bread. Mum watched bemusedly as he devoured it all, but she'd given up asking him how he could put all that lot away without exploding. Sal and Sara ate half a burger each and said things like, "Yuk!" and "You're *disgusting*!" but Olly just grinned evilly at them. Then Dad came in and had his dinner (Olly sneaked a few chips off his plate when he wasn't looking), and it was time to get started on the tree.

The rest of the evening was a glorious riot of mess and glitter and arguments. Even Smug, the family cat, joined in, though his idea of decorating was to see how many baubles (preferably breakable) he could swipe off the tree with a lightning-fast paw. Olly noted carefully how many of the chocolate decorations were hung up. He counted twenty-seven, not including two that he'd quickly unwrapped and eaten when no one was looking. That meant there must be at least ten more still in the kitchen. Mum had probably hidden them. But Olly was *very* good at finding things.

At last the tree was finished and they all stood back to admire it. Olly had to admit it wasn't bad. A bit garish, maybe – there was far too much tinsel and some of the colours clashed horribly. But it would keep Sal and Sara happy. They were only kids, after all.

Mum made an enormous saucepan of hot chocolate and brought in a tray full of steaming mugs.

"Mum, Olly put *five* sugars in his!" Sara said loudly, pointing.

"No, I didn't!" Olly lied, clenching a fist to show her what he'd do if she ratted on him again.

Sara wasn't impressed. "You did!" she argued. "*And* you'll go and scrape out the saucepan later; you always do!"

"Oh, leave him alone," said Dad. "He's just got a healthy appetite. Anyway, if you can't have a bit of a blow-out at Christmas, when can you?"

"Olly's going to blow *up* one day," Sara said

with virtuous disapproval. "He'll go off bang, just like a cracker. There'll be this *huge* explosion, and *BLUUUURGH* – bits of Olly splattered all over the walls!"

"*Yeeuch!*" Sal protested. "Shut up, Sara! Olly's all right." She glanced sidelong, ingratiatingly, at her brother. "What've you got me for Christmas, Olly? Is it something nice?"

"Sweets," said Sara. "Bet you anything. And he'll eat nearly all of them himself, before you get a look-in."

Mum intervened at that point. "Stop it, the lot of you!" she told them. "The way you're going on, Sara, you'll be lucky if Olly gives you anything at all for Christmas." She paused. "That reminds me – we'd better wrap up the relatives' presents and put them under the tree. Gran and Grandad are arriving tomorrow, and Aunt Liz the day after."

"We'll help!" Sara said eagerly.

"You won't," said Mum. "It's bed for you girls, right now."

"Oh Mum!"

"I want to watch—"

"Video it," Mum interrupted firmly. "I said, *bed.*"

When they'd gone, Olly said, trying to sound casual, "I'll give you a hand, shall I, Mum?"

"All right, love, thanks. The presents are in the kitchen cupboard – the bag with the hideous robin on it. You get those, and I'll fetch the wrapping paper."

Yee-haa! thought Olly as he headed for the kitchen. *Perfect chance to take a closer look at those boxes of sweets!* He spent the next five minutes rummaging through the bag (the extra tree decorations were behind it, so he ate another one while he was at it) until Mum called, "Olly? Come on, hurry up!"

"Coming!" *But first, a peek in the fridge; oh, go on, just a quick one.* Olly opened the fridge door, and drooled at what he saw inside. Ham. Chipolatas. Sausage rolls. Mince pies. Cream. Mum must've brought *tonnes* more bags back from the supermarket that he hadn't even seen!

And there, on the bottom shelf, was the turkey.

Olly stared at the turkey. It looked so succulent, sitting there on the big plate with its legs stuck up in the air. He could almost have eaten it raw. He started daydreaming about what sort of stuffing they might have with it. Chestnut, or sage and onion, or apricot and rice... All three was a bit much to hope for, he supposed, so in his mind he plumped for chestnut, his favourite. Roast spuds, sausages, cranberry sauce, peas, gravy... Then Christmas pud for afters, with *lashings* of cream, then—

"Olly, what on *earth* are you doing in there?"

Olly hastily shut the fridge door and hurried back to the sitting-room. "Sorry, Mum," he said breathlessly. "I was just—"

"Gloating over the contents of the fridge," said Dad, who'd heard the door slam. But he was grinning. "Don't panic, Olly. It'll be Christmas Day before you know it, and then you can eat yourself sick."

Olly was *never* sick, no matter how much he devoured. He grinned back. "Can't wait, Dad!"

"The only thing is, I hope that turkey's big enough," said Mum. "There'll be eight of us for dinner."

Olly looked at her in horror, but Dad said serenely, "Don't worry. We've got all that ham and sausage and heaven knows what else; there's enough to feed an army."

There might have been, Olly thought, but was there enough to feed *him*? Now he considered it, the turkey had looked about the same size as last Christmas's. How long had that lasted? He tried to remember. They'd had cold turkey for dinner on Boxing Day, then turkey sandwiches, then turkey curry, and he'd persuaded Mum to make some soup with the bones.

But last year there had only been five of them to eat it. This year, there'd be eight. *Eight!* Nearly twice as many people, which meant only just over half the amount of turkey for each person!

"Mum..." he began worriedly.

But Mum was taking the presents out of the carrier bag, and Dad had switched the TV on, and they weren't listening to him. Olly sighed. Maybe it'd be all right. After all, like Dad said, there was plenty of other food. Ham. Sausage rolls. Christmas pud. He wasn't going to starve.

Feeling better, though still just a *bit* worried, he turned his attention to cutting and wrapping and Sellotaping presents.

"Hi, Gran! Happy Nearly Christmas!" Olly was waiting at the front gate when the car drew up next day, and as soon as Gran got out he enveloped her in a huge hug. He'd learned a long time ago that grandmothers loved that sort of thing. And it gave him a chance to look over her shoulder into the car. There was a suitcase on the back seat, and two large carrier bags, both bulging promisingly.

"Hello, Olly!" Gran gave him a smacking kiss on the cheek. "You've grown since I last saw you!"

She always said that, even if last time was only a week ago. Grandad, getting out on the other side, said, "You have, and more sideways than upwards, I'd say!"

Olly grinned good-naturedly. "Hi, Grandad. Want a hand with those bags?"

He got the chance for a good feel of the carriers as he took them indoors. They were full of parcels, quite a few of which felt delectably the right shape and size for sweet boxes. Olly watched happily as all the packages were taken out and arranged with the others under the tree. Three were labelled for him, one each from Gran and Grandad, and an extra one from them both. OK, so the one from Gran felt like socks, but the other two... He licked his lips.

Then Gran sprang the best surprise of all.

"I hope you don't think we're being rude," she said to Mum, "but with eight of us for Christmas dinner, we did wonder if there'd be enough. Then when we went to the butcher's yesterday, we saw this in the window, so we bought it."

"This... ?" prompted Olly hopefully. Because Grandad had produced a third carrier bag. One he hadn't seen before. A *big* one.

It was a goose. Plucked and trussed and ready for the oven. A whole, enormous *goose*!

Mum was thrilled, especially when Gran added

that she would quite happily cook the goose on Christmas Day. (Though she didn't want to admit it, Mum had never cooked one in her life and hadn't the foggiest where to start.) Dad was delighted, too. And as for Olly...

When (with some difficulty) the goose had been crammed into the fridge, he spent nearly half an hour just staring at it. Mum's cooker had a double oven, so there'd be room for both birds to be roasted on Christmas morning. He happily imagined the smells, the tastes, second helpings, then thirds... No need to worry about there not being enough to go round. Goose *and* turkey! If there was such a thing as heaven, Olly decided, then he was in it right now.

He was brought back to earth with a wallop by Mum coming into the kitchen and yelling at him for standing there with the fridge door wide open. She banned him from the kitchen for at least an hour, but Olly didn't care.

He went back to the sitting-room, ignored Sal and Sara when they flapped their arms and made gobbling noises at him, and steeled himself for an evening of Monopoly. Grandad always wanted to play Monopoly. He loved it, so long as he won, so they usually let him. After a while Sara got bored and Sal sulked because she'd been sent to jail three times in a row, but the others carried on till supper time. Olly had tomato soup *and* cheese on toast (plus a couple of mince pies when no one was looking – well, they had to be sampled, didn't they?) and finally went to bed feeling that everything was right with the world.

He slept for three hours, then woke up feeling hungry. The house was dark and quiet and everyone else was asleep. Olly couldn't stop thinking about the parcels under the tree.

He should have resisted the temptation, of course. Even as he sneaked down the stairs and into the sitting-room, he knew he *should* have resisted. But what the heck? The parcels were addressed to him, after all. It wasn't really cheating; he was just getting one of his presents a bit early, that was all.

Switching on a lamp, he stared down at the pile of colourful packages under the Christmas tree. He'd better not take the big one from Grandad. Too obvious. But the smaller one...

Prod, prod; feel, feel. Prise up the sticky tape at one end, to make sure... Yep. It was sweets! *Brilliant*! Tucking the package under his arm, Olly reached to switch the lamp off again – then paused, his head turning towards the kitchen door. One little peek...? It wouldn't hurt. No one would know. Just to check that he hadn't dreamed it...

He tiptoed into the kitchen and pulled the fridge door open. There was the turkey, and there was the goose. A grin spread across Olly's face and he leaned as far as he could into the fridge.

"You *wait*," he said happily to the two trussed birds. "The day after tomorrow, you're going to be stuffed and cooked, and then I'm going to *eat* you!"

Christmas dinners don't talk, of course, and the birds simply sat there. With a sigh of sheer pleasure Olly shut the fridge door again and crept back upstairs to his room. He ate half the sweets, then hid the box under the bed and fell soundly asleep, to dream of banquets. Life was *good*.

Apart from the fact that she didn't bring a goose, Aunt Liz's arrival on Christmas Eve was like a re-run of Gran and Grandad's. The car, the hugs and kisses, the bags of wrapped-up parcels. The pile under the tree was getting pretty enormous now, which was just as well, as Olly hadn't been able to stop himself from opening (and eating) another of the presents. It had felt like biscuits, it *was* biscuits, and he hadn't noticed until too late that it was supposed to be for Mum. Oh, well. There'd be such a confusion of packages and wrapping paper tomorrow morning, he'd probably get away with it. So Olly ate two chocolate decorations from the tree to console himself (he'd replace them later, if there were any left) and didn't worry too much.

As well as presents, Aunt Liz had brought more contributions to the feast. The one Olly had his eye on from the start was a huge jar of sweet pickle with all sorts of exotic ingredients. Apparently Gran had told Aunt Liz about the goose, so Aunt Liz had bought the exotic pickle to go with it. Yum! Olly managed to dip his finger in and have a taste when no one was around, and when he'd tasted, he opened the fridge again.

"Know what I'm going to do?" he asked the goose (which again, of course, just sat there). "I'm going to have a fork *and* a spoon, and I'm going to go: *Goose – pickle. Goose – pickle.*" He mimed it, shovelling in imaginary mouthfuls and making smacking noises with his lips. "And I'm going to keep on doing it till you're *all* gone!"

"Hi, Olly!" Aunt Liz's voice came from behind him and made him jump. "Getting in training?"

"Something like that." Olly grinned sheepishly,

hoping she hadn't overheard. She'd think he was crackers, talking to the food.

"Looks good, doesn't it?" She peered past him into the fridge. "Not like last year. I was so busy I didn't have time to do any shopping, and I was supposed to be on a diet anyway. Know what I had for Christmas dinner? Fish fingers!"

A look of shocked sympathy spread across Olly's face. "That's *awful!*" he said. Imagine – no turkey, no roast spuds, no pud or cream or mince pies... It gave him the wobbles just to think about it.

"Well, I'm going to make up for it tomorrow," Aunt Liz told him cheerfully. "Bet I'll eat even more than you do."

Olly laughed. "Bet you won't!"

"Well, I'm going to try." She grinned at him. "Unless we get burglars in the night. That happened to one of my neighbours a couple of years ago – someone broke in on Christmas Eve. They stole all the presents, then they raided the fridge and took *everything* in it."

Olly's eyes opened very wide. "You mean, all their Christmas dinner?" he said, aghast.

Aunt Liz nodded. "The lot. It was a real disaster."

It certainly was, Olly thought. In fact he couldn't imagine anything worse in the entire world. And as time went on, the story started to prey more and more on his mind. It wasn't that he thought they *would* get burglars – they weren't going out this evening, and if thieves tried to break in tonight, someone would be sure to wake up. But all the same, it was worrying…

Everyone was supposed to go to bed early on Christmas Eve. As usual the twins didn't want to, and Dad sternly told them that if they didn't, Santa wouldn't come down the chimney.

"Oh, grow up, Dad!" Sara retorted, pulling a face. "What do you think we are, little kids? We've known for *centuries* there's no such thing as Santa!"

"And even if there was," Sal chimed in disdainfully, "we haven't got a chimney, have we?"

Dad muttered gloomily about kids not being like they were in his day, and Mum settled the argument by giving the twins a straight choice between bed and no presents. Sal and Sara went, looking huffy, and Mum said, "You too, Olly. The girls'll wake us all up at some unspeakable hour, so you'd better get some sleep while you can."

"OK, Mum," Olly agreed. "I'll just have a bit of cheese or something." At dinner time Aunt

45

Liz had beaten him to the last baked potato, so he was still hungry.

"Too much cheese gives you indigestion," said Gran, without looking up. "*And* bad dreams."

Yeah, yeah, Olly thought. He grinned pityingly at her. "Sure. 'Night, Gran."

In the kitchen, he made a (very) large cheese sandwich, then checked the fridge one last time, just to be sure everything was all right. It was. So after another voracious gloat over the goose and the turkey, he went up to his room and climbed contentedly into bed.

Olly really should have listened to Gran. He fell asleep all right; no problem. But it wasn't long before Gran's warning about cheese started coming true. Not the indigestion bit – Olly *never* had indigestion.

But he *did* have a dream...

In it, he was prowling through the house, looking for something to eat. Nothing unusual there, except that wherever he looked, he couldn't find a single edible thing. Nothing in the sitting-room, nothing in the bathroom or the twins' bedroom. No one else was in the house, but in the dream that didn't strike Olly as weird. It didn't occur to him, either, that if it was food he wanted, he was looking in all the wrong places.

Until he found himself standing outside a closed but familiar door.

The kitchen – of course! Why hadn't he thought of that before? Telling himself he was a prize idiot, Olly reached out for the door handle.

And paused as he heard voices on the other side.

His first reaction was to feel annoyed. Someone had beaten him to it – several someones, in fact, because it sounded like at least three different people. He couldn't hear what they were saying, but he wasn't interested in that. All that mattered to him was to go in and get *his* share of the goodies before the others scoffed the lot.

He went to grab the handle again.

And stopped again.

Something about the voices wasn't quite right. Olly listened harder. Then realized why he hadn't been able to make out the words. There weren't any words. Whoever was in there wasn't talking; they were just making noises. Very peculiar noises.

Gobble, gobble, said one. *Gobble, gobble,* replied another. And a third one snorted out something that sounded a bit like a laugh, but really was more of a honking squawk.

The truth dawned on Olly. Sal and Sara – this

was just like the noises they'd made the other day, when they were taking the mickey out of him over the turkey. *Cheek!* he thought indignantly. They thought they could sneak into the kitchen and pinch all the food while he was asleep! He'd give them *Gobble, gobble!* He'd have their guts on a plate!

He grabbed the handle, and slammed the door open.

Or tried to. But something on the other side resisted his efforts, and the door would hardly budge. Olly pushed harder. He shoved with all his strength.

A fat, white feather drifted out through the gap and tickled his nose. What on earth...?

Then suddenly the door smacked wide open. Olly stumbled forward –

And plunged face-first into a pulsing, heaving mass of choking whiteness.

"*Aarrmmmmpf!*" It was supposed to be a yell of shock, but it was muffled by feathers – millions of feathers, piling in on him and filling his mouth, his nose, his ears. Olly's arms flailed wildly; he tried to shout again but the feathers were suffocating him, more and more and still more of them, clinging to him, smothering him, burying him under an avalanche. He couldn't scream, couldn't breathe, couldn't *move*.

And echoing horribly through the soft white mass came a huge, deafening sound.

GOBBLE … GOBBLE … GOBBLE …

Olly woke with a yelp of terror, arms waving, legs kicking, to find himself tangled under the folds of his duvet, safe in his own bed.

He shot upright, blinking like an owl, his heart thudding under his ribs. The duvet was still tangled around him and he kicked it off, before lying down again with a huge sigh of relief. What a dream! Must've been the cheese after all, he told himself.

Oh, well. It was over now. And it *was* just a dream. Nothing to be scared of. Best thing was to forget it and go back to sleep.

He lay down again, telling himself that he wasn't really hungry. He was just about to shut his eyes when he heard a noise from downstairs.

Olly froze, listening. The noise had sounded suspiciously like breaking glass. And now there were other sounds. Furtive. As if someone was moving around very, very quietly…

Olly's mind shot back to Aunt Liz's story about the burglars, and his mouth dropped open in horror. *Someone was breaking into the house! And they were in the kitchen!*

He was out of bed in one second flat, and heading for the door. The landing was dark, but

Olly knew his way around by feel, and he crept to the top of the stairs, where he paused to listen again.

There *was* someone down there. He could hear a shuffle, like cautious footsteps. And then came a *clink*, as if knives and forks were being taken out of a drawer.

Olly thought: *The food!* And, forgetting everything else, he started to run down the stairs.

The kitchen door was shut, but there was a light showing underneath. Olly wasn't the least bit scared. All he felt was a towering fury at the burglars who were about to steal his Christmas dinner. He'd show them! He'd *get* them!

With a single dramatic movement, he flung the door open.

And stopped dead, eyes widening in astonishment, at the sight that confronted him.

The kitchen was hung with decorations. There were paper chains, mobiles, baubles – everything you could possibly think of. The table had been pulled into the middle of the room, and Mum's festive Christmas tablecloth was spread over it.

And on the table was *food*.

In all his life Olly had never seen a feast like it. There was a dish piled high with roast potatoes, golden-brown and glistening. There was another dish overflowing with Brussels sprouts and chestnuts. There were glazed carrots, chipolata sausages, stuffings (sage and onion, chestnut, *and* apricot and rice), cranberry sauce (for the turkey), apple sauce (for the goose), a huge jug of gravy. And that was just the main course. At one end of the table, the biggest Christmas pud Olly could have imagined sat round and fat and juicy, with custard oozing down it and a sprig of holly stuck in the top. An enormous pile of mince pies teetered next to a bowl of luscious cream, and beyond them was a vast iced and decorated cake.

The sight and the wonderful mingled smells of the banquet hit Olly's senses so blissfully that for a few moments he didn't notice that there was something missing. But then he saw, right in the middle of the table, one empty dish. It was the biggest one of all: an oval china carving dish. The carving knife and fork lay neatly to one side of it. On the other side, unopened, stood Aunt Liz's jar of exotic pickle.

And finally, the last sight registered on Olly's brain.

There were figures sitting round the table. They all had place settings – cutlery, glass, cracker, serviette with holly and robins on it.

They were all wearing paper hats. And they were all looking at Olly where he stood paralysed in the doorway.

Olly stared back, disbelieving. Then, like a ghastly chorus, the "dinner guests" all said together, "Merry Christmas, Olly!"

Olly's mouth started to open and shut like a stranded fish. He tried to back away, but his legs weren't working properly, and he had to grab the door-frame to steady himself.

Because the people sitting round the table weren't people at all.

They were...

They were...

Shock hit Olly so hard that he went dizzy. The scene in front of him wavered. The floor under his feet seemed to tilt...

And he slumped in a dead faint to the floor.

"Mmmm ... pass the potatoes, please."

"More sausages for me."

"Who's got the carrots? Yum!"

Olly came to slowly and woozily as the buzz of voices started to make sense. Potatoes ... sausages ... carrots... He must have dozed off, and the family had started Christmas dinner without him.

"Chestnut stuffing..." he mumbled, without

opening his eyes. "I'm going to have chestnut stuffing..."

A voice he didn't recognize said, "Of course you are, Olly. Of *course* you are!" There were sniggers round the table. Olly tried to join in, though he didn't quite know why. The sniggers hadn't sounded very pleasant.

"You'd better not have eaten all the sage and onion," he said. "I want some of that, too."

This time there was a significant sort of silence. Olly's eyes were still shut, and he still felt a bit too wonky to open them, or even to move. His head hurt. Had he banged it or was it just a headache? He hardly ever got headaches. He wasn't going down with the flu, was he?

"Mum..." he said.

"She's not here," someone told him. Again, he didn't recognize the voice. "No one's here, Olly. Except us. And you."

Huh? thought Olly. What was that supposed to mean? This was crazy; he must still be half asleep, or something. Better make himself wake up properly.

He tried to sit up.

And couldn't. Something was holding him down.

Huh? said his mind again. His legs seemed to

be stuck together. His arms, too. He couldn't move.

Olly made an inarticulate gargling noise, and opened his eyes.

The first thing he saw was the kitchen ceiling. It was dead ahead of him, and it took him a couple of seconds to realize that he was, in fact, lying on his back. His back felt cold, too. He wasn't in bed, or on the sofa or even the carpet. This felt too solid. Like stone.

Or china.

"What's going on?" he demanded. "Where am I?"

"Merry Christmas, Olly."

"Yeah. Merry Christmas!"

"Best ever, if you ask me."

"For us. Don't know about *him*, though!"

More sniggers. Olly's brain was still a bit fuzzy, but he didn't recognize any of the voices. Who *were* all these people? He couldn't remember what had happened to him, and in sudden panic he turned his head.

And screamed.

"Hey!" said one of the figures at the table, sounding aggrieved. "Keep the noise down, will you?"

Olly tried to scream again, but not a single croak came out. Because what he was looking at was too horrible to be believed.

He was looking straight into the face of a giant turkey which was wearing a paper hat and holding a knife and fork in its wing feathers.

The turkey's beak clacked open and it said, "That's better!"

On the other side of the table something grunted, "Pass the sauce."

"Which one?" said the turkey.

"Cranberry. Oooh ... no; the pickle. I've *got* to try that!"

Olly jerked his head the other way. There was a pig sitting on the chair. A pig the size of a horse. It, too, was wearing a paper hat. And grasped in one of its trotters was a Christmas cracker.

Olly could feel the panic coming. It was like standing on a railway line and watching an express train heading straight for him. "No..." he garbled. "No, oh no, oh *no*..."

"Oh, shut up!" said the turkey. "Here, have an apple."

A wing came out and popped something into Olly's gaping mouth. It was an apple, all right. He'd seen pictures of grand banquets in the olden days. They use to roast apples, then put them in the mouths of pigs.

Pigs that were about to be *eaten*.

"Mmmpfffhoowhff!" he spluttered, trying to

spit the apple out and struggling to get his arms and legs free. But the apple didn't budge, and he still couldn't move a muscle.

And in one terrifying flash he remembered exactly what it was that had made him faint.

The "dinner guests" at the groaning kitchen table were gigantic birds and animals. There was a turkey. A pig. A goose. A chicken. A cow. They all had paper hats on, and they were all leaning forward to leer and grin at him where he lay in the middle of the table.

Christmas dinner was ready. And Olly was the main course.

"*Mmmmghh!*" He yelped hoarsely as a fork prodded him in the thigh.

"Hey, look at that!" said the goose, which had cold blue eyes with a hungry glitter in them. "All plump and juicy! Lovely!"

"Everyone got veg?" the cow asked. "Right – let's dish him up, then!"

Olly writhed and squirmed. *NO, NO, NO...* He chomped desperately on the apple but still couldn't shift it.

"Put some gravy on him first," the pig suggested. "I *love* gravy."

Olly shut his eyes in sheer terror as the gravy jug sailed over his head. Down it came, pouring in a thick, warm, glutinous stream that ran over his chest and stomach, down his arms, into his hair. He could even smell its rich, savoury aroma.

"Ahh!" said the pig happily. "Yum, *yum!*"

The last shred of Olly's nerve snapped, and with the most enormous effort he'd ever made in his life, he spat the apple out of his mouth. It bounced across the table and landed in the cream bowl, and Olly's voice rose in a scream that nearly lifted the ceiling.

"*NO-O-O-O-O-O!!!*"

Everything stopped. No one moved, no one said a word, but all the creatures round the table stared down at him in surprise.

Then: "Charming!" said the cow.

"He ought to learn some manners," commented the goose, who was still holding the gravy jug.

"Ignore him," said the pig. "I'm hungry!"

Olly found his voice again. "But – but – but –" he yammered. "You can't eat me!"

Silence again. They all looked blank, and at last the turkey asked, "Why not?"

"B-b-because ... I'm *human!*"

"So?" said the turkey.

"It's all *wrong!*" Olly protested desperately. "I'm human and you're animals – *I'm* supposed to eat *you*, not the other way round! I mean – I mean, you're vegetarians!"

"I'm not," said the pig, sounding insulted.

"We eat insects," said the goose, nodding at the turkey and the chicken. "They're not vegetables, are they?"

The cow shrugged. "And I'll try anything once. Why not? Specially if it looks as tasty as you do."

"Anyway," said the pig, "you're a fine one to talk, aren't you? We've all been *watching* you these last few days, and we've seen the way you eat. People call *me* a pig...!" It made a snorting, grunting noise of disgust.

"What do you mean, you've all been watching me?" asked Olly, trying hard not to panic again. "How could you have done? You weren't here!"

The pig sighed. "Weren't we? What did you have for dinner last night?"

Olly thought back. "Chicken nuggets..."

"Right. And the night before?"

A gulp. Olly looked nervously at the cow. "Beefburgers..."

"There you are, then. And your folks have got turkey and goose ready for Christmas dinner. And ham, and sausages. *Pork* sausages." The pig leered at him, showing fangs. "Get the picture?"

Olly got the picture.

58

"All us animals to pig out on," the goose chimed in, then held up a wing to the pig. "Sorry..." The pig nodded, and the goose continued. "We've had enough, Olly. Now, it's *our* turn to be greedy. We want *our* Christmas dinner."

"And you," said the turkey triumphantly, "are *it!*"

The animal faces leaned, ogling and drooling, over Olly. "Know what I'm going to do?" said the goose, with relish. "I'm going to open this jar of pickle, have a fork *and* a spoon, and I'm going to go: *Olly – pickle. Olly – pickle.* And I'm going to keep on doing it till you're *all* gone!"

"No!" Olly pleaded. "No, *please...*"

"Serve him up!" said the pig.

"A nice bit of front leg for me!" said the cow.

"Sage and onion!"

"Chestnuts!"

"Apricot and rice!"

"Yum, *yum!*"

"Gobble, gobble, till he's all gone!"

"Yeah! Gobble, gobble... Gobble, GOBBLE ... GOBBLE, **GOBBLE...**"

"Olly!"

"Come on, Olly! It's Christmas!"

"Whuh? Wha?" With a snuffling gasp Olly opened his eyes again. There was the ceiling. There were two faces looming over him...

"No-o-o –" he began.

"Hey, lazybones, wake *up!*" The faces slipped into focus and became the grinning forms of Sal and Sara.

"Come on, Olly!" Sara thumped his chest with a clenched fist. "You've missed breakfast!"

"And we want our presents!" Sal added.

He was in his room. In bed. Not on a china dish. No giant animals, no laden table. Just his twin sisters. Now Sara was sitting on his legs while Sal twisted his arm.

"Come on, come on!"

"Lazy pig!"

"*Don't call me that!*" Olly said in horror. "Get off me!" He scrabbled out of bed, pushing them away, out of the room, then stood there in his pyjamas, trying to stop shaking. It had been a dream. Just a *dream*.

Outside the door, the twins were giggling. "Come on, Olly!" Sal called again. "Or you'll miss dinner, too! Turkey and goose!"

"Honk, honk! Gobble, gobble!"

"*SHUT UP!*" Olly screamed. He didn't want to *hear* those noises, ever again!

Still laughing, the girls pounded away down

the landing. Olly got dressed. Very unsteadily. He went downstairs. Very slowly.

"Merry Christmas, Olly!" everyone greeted him, and Mum added, "We saved your breakfast."

Olly had to steel himself to go into the kitchen. But it was all right. Everything was normal: the two birds had gone from the fridge, and there was a wonderful smell coming from the oven.

At least, he'd have thought it was wonderful yesterday.

He switched on the kettle. All he wanted was a cup of coffee, nothing else. When the water boiled he made his drink, and was stirring it when, behind him, he heard a noise. Just a little one. But unmistakable.

"*Honk...*"

Olly whipped round. There was nobody else in the room.

Then: "*Gobble, gobble...*"

It came from the direction of the oven. And it sounded ... *menacing.*

Olly turned white, then scarlet, then white again. He was staring at the oven door, transfixed, when Mum came in.

"Come on, dreamy!" she said cheerfully. "At this rate we won't get the presents opened before dinner's ready." She smiled at him. "I bet you can't wait to tuck in!"

Olly swallowed, very hard. "Actually, Mum," he said in a small voice, "I don't think I'm going to be very hungry..."

Jungle Bells

"Grace! Grace, where are you? *Grace!*"

Sophie hissed her kid sister's name as she scurried furtively along yet another turning in the maze of paths that wound between the cages and enclosures. She didn't dare call any louder. The zoo had officially closed half an hour ago and all the other visitors had gone, but she'd bet anything that the keepers were still here. Grace (*Disgrace* would have been a better name for her, Sophie told herself) had got into enough trouble with the keepers already. Mocking the orang-utans, banging on the glass in the aquarium (right next to a sign that said DO NOT TOUCH THE GLASS), trying to climb into the giraffes' enclosure, feeding chocolate to the elephants... If they caught her doing anything else, they'd probably throw her *and* Sophie to the lions.

Sophie stopped to get her breath and look around. She was tired, angry, freezing cold ... and, now, just a little bit scared. Where *was* Grace? She'd lost her sense of direction; with dusk closing in, all the paths looked the same. And there was something creepy about the empty paths, the silent cages, the deserted kiosks. The zoo's cheerful atmosphere had changed, and Sophie didn't like it one bit.

She shivered, and thought bitterly: *What a way to spend Christmas Eve!* But Mum had insisted. Grace was driving her completely mad – "Where are my presents? I want my presents *now!*" etc., etc. – and Mum had told Sophie to take her to the zoo, like it or lump it. You didn't argue with Mum when she was in that sort of mood. So they'd gone. And it had been sheer torture. And now Grace had completely vanished, and Sophie was tearing around like a demented bluebottle, trying to find her. Only the thought of Mum's wrath stopped her from stomping straight home and leaving Grace to the mercy of the keepers.

At least ... if there *were* any keepers. It occurred to Sophie suddenly that she hadn't actually seen one for quite a while, and a cold, prickly feeling crawled over her skin. They couldn't all have gone, could they? Checked the cages, locked up the gates and gone home?

Her heart started to thump under her ribs. It was very, very quiet and, apart from the globes on tall poles that dimly illuminated the paths, she couldn't see any lights. There were no sounds of voices or clanging doors or clanking buckets – nothing at all. It was beginning to look horribly as if there was no one else here.

So, even if she did find Grace, how on earth were they going to get out?

"Grace," she said through clenched teeth (clenched because otherwise they'd have started chattering), "when I get my hands on you..."

The thought of what she'd do vanished when she suddenly heard something in the distance. Music – it sounded like a disco! And over on the far side of the zoo were lights – a cluster of them: red, blue, green, yellow...

There *were* people still here! With a gasp of relief, Sophie hurried down the paths towards the lights and the music. She ran past the gorillas' cage, then, as she went round the corner by the big cats' enclosures, a small figure detached itself from the shadows of the bushes and shot away down a side turning.

"*Grace!*" Sophie's voice went up in a screech

of outrage as her little sister darted across her path. Forgetting the lights, she took off in pursuit. She could just see Grace ahead of her, pelting along for all she was worth; but Sophie was much bigger and much faster, and as Grace skidded round another corner, she caught up, and pounced.

"*Owww!*" Grace yelled furiously. "Get off me, you big bully!"

Sophie grabbed her under the armpits and lifted her off her feet. Grace kicked madly, but she hung on. "What d'you think you're playing at, you little monster? I've been looking all over for you; the zoo shut half an hour ago, and—"

"Hey! Hume!"

The voice came from a nearby clump of shrubs, and Sophie nearly jumped out of her skin. Dropping Grace, she spun round.

There was no one else there.

Sophie shook her head. She was imagining things; must be. Got herself so steamed up that her brain was playing tricks. She whirled back to Grace. Grace hadn't run away but was standing her ground. And *smirking*.

Then from the darkness by one of the cages, a second voice announced: "Arrrr-*hem!*"

"*Aah!*" Sophie jumped again, even more violently.

The voice said, "Yes, you, Hume! What are you doing to our friend?"

A bulky shadow moved by the cage. Then a shape appeared out of the dark.

And Sophie found herself face to face with a polar bear.

It stood on all fours in the middle of the path, head down, its white fur glimmering in the eerie light of the globe-lamps. It was staring straight at her, and it did *not* look pleased.

"Aah ... baa ... gaaa..." Sophie could only make noises. She thought she was going to faint. Then she thought she was going to be sick.

"Well?" said the polar bear. "I asked you nicely. What are you doing to the green cub?"

"G-g-g-green cub...?" Grace was wearing a green coat and leggings, Sophie thought wildly. "Sh-she's your f-f-f-f...?"

"Friend. That's what I said. So leave her alone."

"That's right," said a second voice at her back. Sophie spun round as if someone had thumped her. Less than two metres from where she stood were two gorillas. One of them had a brightly wrapped parcel under its arm; the other one was scratching its head. Then a group of chimps came up behind the gorillas. And other creatures were emerging out of the dusk. Lions. Tigers. Zebras. Camels. Wolves. The vast, grey bulk of an elephant. Most of them carried parcels, too, in their hands or their mouths. And the elephant had a red bow tied round its trunk. They gathered round Sophie in a tight, menacing circle, and every one of them stared accusingly at her.

Sophie felt as if the entire world was turning upside down. She was dreaming this, she must be, she *must*...

The polar bear looked at Grace. "Do you know her?" it asked.

Grace scowled. "She's my sister. She's *horrible*."

"I'm not!" Sophie protested desperately. "I'm nice, honestly I am!"

"Yeah?" a lion with an enormous mane growled through a mouthful of parcel. "Then why were you clawing and snarling at the green cub?"

Sophie looked wildly around the circle of animals. "I wasn't!" she babbled. "I just ... just..."

"It looked like clawing and snarling to me," said a terrifyingly large and stripy tiger. "And that's *not* nice."

"Like Polar Bear said, she's our friend," the

70

elephant added, in a rumbling tone that shook the tarmac under Sophie's feet.

"Yeah," agreed the lion. "We *like* her. She opened all our doors for us."

"*What?*" Sophie squealed. "Grace, you didn't!"

"Did!" Grace smirked.

"How?"

Grace shrugged. "Magicked them. You can, on Christmas Eve."

"But – but – "

"That's right," said the elephant. "It's a magic night, you see. We always come out of our cages on Christmas Eve."

"Only we need a bit of help," supplied the tiger.

"Yeah," said the gorilla with the parcel. "We can't get the doors open by ourselves. So we have to find a Hume to do it for us."

"One young enough to believe in magic, and old enough not to tell," finished the elephant. "Then when we get out, we can have our party."

"P-p-p-*party?*" Sophie stammered. The disco? The lights? Surely they couldn't mean...?

The tiger looked at Grace. "Not very bright, your sister, is she?"

"She can't help it," said a giraffe, which had just joined the crowd and loomed over Sophie like a crane. It bent its head to stare pityingly at her, and continued, quite kindly, "It's very simple, dear. You Humes have Christmas parties, don't you?"

"Y-y-y…" Sophie couldn't manage a complete "Yes", but the giraffe got the idea.

"There you are then. We animals have them, too. A bit of music, a bit of a sing-song, some presents – just like you. Only we have to keep quiet about it, you see. If the keepers knew what was going on, they'd put a stop to it."

"Not to mention what they'd do if they found out we can talk," the lion added.

"Well, tonight we can, anyway," said the giraffe. "That's another part of the magic." Its long neck swung round and it looked at all the other animals. "And it's part of the problem, too. We know the little green Hume cub won't tell on us. But what about this one?"

"Hmm." The gorilla studied Sophie in a way that made her quake in her shoes. "Good point. I mean, we can't afford to take chances, can we?"

"We could eat her," the tiger suggested brightly. "Solve the problem in one gulp, so to speak."

Grace sniggered, and Sophie's hair stood on end.

"Or I could spray her with lots of water," said the elephant. "It'd freeze in this weather, and she couldn't make much trouble from inside a block of ice."

"We know, we know!" piped up some new voices. Sophie looked down, and saw a gaggle of meerkats bouncing up and down near her feet. Some of them had bows on, too. "Bury her in a flower-bed!" they squeaked. "We'll dig the hole, we're good at that!"

Sophie's self-control snapped. "No!" she yelped. "Please! I won't tell on you, I promise I won't!"

The animals mumbled and murmured and growled among themselves, chewing this over.

"She's only a cub…"

"But you can't always trust the big Hume cubs…"

Sophie bent her knees, trying to make herself look smaller.

"She did say *promise*…"

"I know, but…"

"She's our friend's sister…"

"True. But I never liked *my* sisters…"

The polar bear cleared its throat with a roar that silenced all the muttering. "I think," it said, "that we should ask the green cub what *she* thinks." It turned to Grace. "Well, green cub? Can we trust her?"

Grace studied Sophie, and in that moment Sophie remembered all the awful things they'd ever said and done to each other. Her heart began to sink. She began to shiver.

"Grace ... please?" she begged in a very small voice.

"We-ell..." said Grace.

"Pretty please?"

Grace stuck a finger in her mouth and looked thoughtful. Then suddenly she demanded, "What have you got me for Christmas?"

"Uh?" said Sophie.

"You heard. What have you got me for Christmas?"

"Well, I – er – " Sophie gulped. "A bubble watch." It had been in a sale and cost her all of one pound fifty.

Grace scowled. "*Boring*. I want a pair of rollerblades."

"*What?*" Sophie screeched. "Do you know how much they *cost*?"

Grace nodded, grinning, and Sophie got the message. This was pure blackmail. Either she saved up to get Grace the blades, or Grace would tell the animals not to trust her. And that could only mean...

"Yes!" she promised frantically. "I'll do it, I'll save up!"

"Promise?"

Sophie could feel dozens of pairs of eyes boring into her, and dozens of pairs of ears listening very carefully indeed. She swallowed, hard. "Promise," she said.

Grace looked triumphantly at her, then turned to the polar bear and announced, "OK. She won't tell." She glanced at Sophie again, meaningfully. "'Cos if she does…"

A chorus of assenting growls or rumbles or grunts finished the warning for her.

"Never mind, bigger Hume cub," said the giraffe. "It *is* Christmas, after all. Season of Goodwill, and all that."

"…es," Sophie managed. She shut her eyes. "Please … can we go home now?"

"Home?" Grace echoed indignantly. "No way! *I* want to go to the party!"

Sophie's mouth dropped open in alarm at the thought of what *that* would do to her frazzled nerves. She was frantically trying to think of a way to change Grace's mind, when the polar bear said sorrowfully, "Well … we'd love to invite you, of course, green cub."

"Specially after what you did for us," the giraffe added.

"Quite. But … it wouldn't be *right*, you see.

It's an *animals'* party, and for Humes, it – well, it might be a bit…"

"Dangerous," said the gorilla.

"Exactly. Some of us are pretty big, and when the fun really gets going, we get excited."

The elephant nodded. "Just think if I trod on you by accident," it said. "I'd feel *awful*."

Not half as awful as we'd feel, Sophie thought. Her mind conjured up a picture of break-dancing hippos and she pushed it away very quickly.

Grace's mouth turned down at the corners. "But I *want* to go," she insisted.

"We know. But it really is much safer not to. Look," the polar bear said consolingly, "I know you're disappointed, but if you go on home, then maybe – just maybe – we might be able to do … well, *something* nice for you."

Grace's expression started to change. "What sort of something?"

"Ohh … don't know yet. You'll have to wait and see. But it *will* be nice. Promise."

Grace gave in. Maybe, Sophie thought, she was bright enough to see the sense in what the animals were saying. And the promise of a surprise cheered her up, so the idea of missing the party wasn't so bad after all. Anyway, they had a grand escort to the zoo gates. Grace rode on the polar bear, and all the other animals followed in a long procession. One of the gorillas offered Sophie a piggy-back, but she only turned pale and said, "No, thankyou, thankyouverymuch."

At the gates, the elephant picked them up, one after the other, in its trunk, and lifted them dizzyingly over the top. When they were both on the pavement outside, a chimp popped its head above the gate, winked, and said, "Bye then, Humes! You take good care, now!"

From behind the gate came an assortment of cheerful noises. "Yeah! Bye, Humes! And thanks again, little green cub!"

Sophie looked at Grace. Grace looked at Sophie. "Yellow ones," she said firmly.

"Uh?" Sophie blinked dazedly.

"My rollerblades. I want yellow ones."

"Oh. Oh, right. Yeah. I … uh … won't forget." She wouldn't *dare*.

They walked along the street towards the bus stop. Grace was very quiet. Sophie couldn't hear the music now, and she started to wonder if the whole episode had been some kind of mad waking dream. Talking animals, zoo parties, bows and presents… It was completely insane, wasn't it? It hadn't *really* happened?

By the time they got home, she didn't know

what she really did think about it all. Grace behaved herself all evening, putting Mum in a good mood, and Sophie was extremely glad to fall into bed and try to forget the entire crazy thing.

Until, in what seemed to be the middle of the night, she woke up with a yelp of shock to find someone shaking her violently.

"Sophie! Sophie, get up, get up!"

"What?" Sophie sat up dizzily. "*Grace!* What d'you think you're doing – what sort of time do you call this?"

"Don't know, don't care!" Grace slammed the bedside lamp on, hurting Sophie's eyes. She was quivering with excitement. "Get up! Come into the garden and see!"

"See what, for crying out loud?"

"In the *garden! Come on!*"

Sophie was furious – but Grace was determined, and when Grace was determined, no one had any peace until she'd got what she wanted. She bounced with impatience while Sophie struggled into some clothes, then all but dragged her along the landing, down the stairs and outside through the back door.

"Look, look!" Grace had a torch and she shone it across the lawn. Sophie started to say angrily, "If Mum knew you'd been prancing around out here in the middle of the night—"

And stopped, staring.

"See?" Grace hissed triumphantly.

There were things on the grass. All over the grass, in fact. Sophie blinked, hardly able to take it all in. There were coloured streamers, shimmering and fluttering in the wind. There were daft cardboard hats. There were party poppers. And there was one very large red bow. Sophie had seen that bow before.

Round the elephant's trunk.

"They came!" Grace crowed. "They didn't forget! And look, they've left us a present!"

They certainly had. In the middle of all the cheerful chaos was a parcel, extremely badly wrapped in extremely garish Christmas paper. A large label on it said, HAPY CRISSMAS HUME CUBBS, with the letters all wonky and some of them backwards, as if whoever had written it couldn't spell and wasn't very good at holding a crayon either.

Grace pounced on the parcel and tore the paper open. Inside were two oranges, three apples, a squashy banana, a handful of hay, a chunk of steak and half a sardine. Sophie goggled, completely baffled, but Grace knew exactly what the animals meant.

"Christmas dinner!" she squealed delightedly.

"They're sharing their Christmas dinner with us!"

There was something else tucked in among all the food. Small and flat and square... Gingerly, Sophie pulled it out and, in the torchlight, stared at it.

It was a CD. The picture on the cover showed a whole crowd of creatures leaping around under disco lights – complete, Sophie noticed, with break-dancing hippos. Splashed across it was a title: THE BEASTLY BALL – MEGA-MUSIC FOR MONSTER MERRIMENT!

"It's their disco album!" Grace squealed. *"Brilliant!"*

Sophie swallowed very hard. She looked at the CD again. Then she stared round at the streamers and hats and all the other party bits strewn on the lawn. Then she thought about her parents. She couldn't explain this away to them. Not in a million years. She couldn't even explain it to herself.

"Come on," she said to Grace. "We'd better pick this lot up and hide them before Mum and Dad wake up."

Grace grinned. "I'm going to keep them *all*. Well ... maybe not the meat and the sardine."

"Right," said Sophie. "Yeah. Right."

As they crept back into the house with armfuls

of streamers, Grace looked sideways, craftily at Sophie.

"They kept their promise, didn't they?"

Sophie nodded. She couldn't think of a sensible reply.

Grace grinned with triumphant satisfaction. "*Yellow* rollerblades," she said.

Feed the Birds

"Brr!" Nicky whirled in through the back door and slammed it behind her with a resounding crash. "It's *freezing* out there!"

Her brother, Pete, who was making himself a sandwich, peered disconsolately out of the kitchen window. "Be all right if it snowed," he grumbled. "But you can't do anything in this except hang around indoors. It's boring."

"Well, I hope it doesn't snow. I hate it." Nicky dumped two carrier bags thankfully on the kitchen floor, and Pete said curiously, "What on earth's in that one? It looks like it weighs a tonne."

"It does. *And* the bus didn't come, so I had to lug it up from town."

"What is it, then?"

Nicky looked a bit sheepish. "You'll laugh."

"Don't know yet, do I?"

"Well ... I was thinking about the birds. You know that talk we had at school – the guy from the Wildlife Trust? He said the creatures that live in gardens have a hard time trying to survive in bad weather, and if people put food out for them it'd save lots of their lives..."

Pete's eyebrows went up. "You mean, that dead weight's *bird* food?"

Nicky went pink. "Well ... yeah. Don't look at me like that! It's about nine million below zero out there – even the TV and papers have been saying people ought to help the birds. I'm just doing my bit." She puffed and grunted as she heaved the carrier on to the table. "Anyway, this stuff was half price, but only if you bought a big bag. So I did; so there."

She pulled the carrier open. Pete stared at what was revealed.

"That," he said incredulously, "is *bird food*?"

Nicky shrugged. "It's only vegetable dye. The woman in the shop said so. I expect they do it so the birds can see it better, or something. Look; there's all different seeds, and little pellets."

"And what are those electric blue bits? And the bright pink ones? And the bilious green?"

"Oh, how should I know? It's all good for them, the woman—"

"In the shop said so; OK, OK. How much did you pay for it?"

"A fiver." Nicky saw his expression and added defensively, "Like I said, you had to have the biggest size to get it for half price."

Pete was horrified. "You spent five pounds of your own money on sparrows and blackbirds? That's it: you really *are* barking mad!" Then he remembered something. "Hang on – you told me this morning that you only had seventy-five pee! So where did a fiver come from, all of a sudden?"

"I ... sort of borrowed it. Out of the shopping money Mum gave me."

"Oh, brilliant! So what if she kicks up?"

"She won't. You know what Mum's like about ecology; she'll probably pay for it herself."

"You hope! One look at that stuff and she'll more likely throw the whole lot in the dustbin! Honestly, Nicky, you're nuts."

Nicky shrugged again. "Well, I've done it now, haven't I? I don't suppose they'd take it back."

"They might. Where did you get it – the garden shop?"

"No. There's a new place opened up in that side street, past the bookshop. They sell things for pets – food and toys and flea powder and everything, and wild animal food, too."

"Yeah?" Pete said in surprise. "There was no sign of any new shop there last week."

"I know. They must have moved in really fast. The shop's a bit small and weird, but the woman there was really nice."

"I bet she was, taking five quid off you!" Then suddenly Pete grinned. "Oh, well. I suppose it's in a good cause, isn't it?"

"Course it is. And if you're so bored, you can do a bit of birdwatching now, can't you?"

"Me, a twitcher? Thanks a bunch!" said Pete.

To Nicky's relief, Mum was happy to pay for the bird food. The latest newscasts warned that there was going to be no let-up in the freezing weather, and the ground was rock-hard with frost. Mum agreed that the birds needed all the help they could get, and Nicky was "very thoughtful and responsible" (Nicky ignored Pete's whispered remarks about toadying). She was, however, a bit dubious when she first saw the bag.

"Those colours really are horrendously garish," she said. "*I* certainly wouldn't eat anything that looked like that! Are you *sure* there's nothing harmful in it, Nicky?"

"Honestly, Mum, it's completely safe," Nicky assured her.

"The woman in the shop said so," added Pete, keeping a dead straight face.

Nicky aimed a backwards kick at him but missed. "I'll go and put some outside, shall I?" she said.

"Yes, do," Mum agreed. "Put it on the grass just beyond the patio. Then you can watch the birds from the living-room window."

The lawn looked weird with the bird food scattered on it. Nicky had to admit that the colours really were pretty awful. "But at least we can see when it's all gone, so we'll know when to put down some more."

"If I haven't been carted off to Casualty with a migraine by then," Pete teased.

"Oh, shut up! No one's making you look at it."

He shrugged. "Might as well take the risk. There's nothing else to do."

It didn't take the birds long to start investigating the food, and soon they were arriving in large numbers. This was a very quiet lane, with only a few houses spaced widely apart, and farmland on both sides, and Nicky guessed that she was probably the only person putting anything out for them at all. They must have been getting pretty desperate, and she was glad to feel that she was helping.

Pete joined her as she watched the birds from the living-room window.

"What's that one with the speckly front?" he said, pointing.

"A thrush." Nicky knocked his hand away. "Don't wave like that; you'll scare them off."

"They won't notice. They're much more interested in stuffing their beaks. Those little ones are sparrows; even I know that. And the black one's a blackbird."

"No it isn't; it's a starling. Blackbirds have got orange beaks unless they're females, and females are brown, not black. Look, here come more starlings. They always go around in flocks."

"Mob-handed, huh?" Pete put on a Chicago gangster voice. "Hey, look at that thrush going for the blue bits! He loves those."

"It's nearly all gone already," said Nicky. "I'll have to get some more in a few minutes."

The birds certainly did like the new food. As Mum put it when she peered out, they were all but queuing up for their shares. Within an hour it was all gone. The birds flew away from the lawn, but they didn't go far. When Nicky went outside with the bag, she could see them in the bare branches of the hedge and shrubs, fluttering and hopping, as if they were waiting for second helpings. And she'd hardly shut the back door before the first ones flew down again.

"Look, the bluetits are coming now," she told Pete. "They don't usually like feeding on the ground. And – oh, *look*, Pete! That little brown one with the turned-up tail – it's a wren!"

Pete wasn't impressed. "Is that supposed to be a big deal, or something?"

"You hardly *ever* see wrens round here. I didn't even know we had any." Enraptured, Nicky wriggled her chair closer to the window, pressing her nose against the glass. Pete sighed. This was boring. Apart from a few with interesting colours or markings, all the birds looked pretty much the same to him.

"I'm going to see what's on TV," he said.

"Suit yourself. I'm staying here."

"Twitcher!" said Pete, and dodged the cushion she threw at him.

By the time it got dark, the birds had demolished four helpings of the food, and Nicky had spent the entire afternoon watching them do it. She'd had a fascinating time. She'd counted twelve different kinds of bird, from the usual sparrows and blackbirds and robins (which for once weren't squabbling with each other the way robins usually did) to some that she simply couldn't recognize. Most exciting of all was when a small flock of vividly coloured little birds, red and black and yellow harlequin, came swooping and twittering to join the feast. Nicky had never seen anything like them before. No one else in the family knew what they were, either, so she resolved to go to the library on her way home from school on Monday and get a bird book.

The next day, Nicky put food out six times before dusk. Lots more birds came; she even saw a magpie and a couple of rooks strutting around. They tried to bully the smaller birds, but the little ones seemed to think there was safety in numbers, and wouldn't be driven away. There was plenty for all, though, so eventually the scuffles settled down.

On Monday morning, Nicky was woken by the sound of sparrows cheeping outside her window. They were perched on the gutter, sitting in a row like little old men on park benches, just as if they knew where the food was coming from and were waiting for more. Downstairs, Nicky looked dubiously at the bag. It was only about two-thirds full now, and she realized that at this rate it wasn't going to last much longer.

"Don't worry," Mum said when she pointed it out. "When it's gone, I'll give you the money for another one. And I'll feed them today while you're at school."

"They'll all get so fat they won't be able to fly," Pete commented. "Then the local cats'll get them."

Mum told him to stop being silly and get on with his breakfast or he'd miss the bus. Nicky put the day's first helping out on the lawn before she left for school, and as she went out of the gate the sparrows and a pair of blackbirds were already fluttering down. She smiled. It felt good to be helping the wildlife.

As she'd promised herself, Nicky got a bird book from the library. The detour meant she was home later than usual; to her disappointment it was dusk by the time she got back, and the birds had all roosted for the night.

"Never mind," Mum said consolingly. "They've all had plenty to eat, which is what really matters. And you've got the book, so tomorrow you'll be able to identify all the unusual ones." She grinned. "I hardly got anything done today, I was so absorbed in watching them. You get to see which ones are bossy, and which ones are cunning – they're a real comedy turn."

Nicky looked at the bag of food. It wasn't

much more than half full now. "Birds?" Pete said when she showed him. "Pigs is more like it!"

She ignored him, and spent all evening reading the bird book. By bedtime she'd gone through it from cover to cover and was beginning to feel quite an expert. The harlequin birds, she discovered, were goldfinches. And Mum described something "like a small thrush but with reddy-brown patches" that she decided was a redwing – a winter visitor. It seemed that the food was attracting a lot of birds that didn't normally come to the garden. Either that, or she'd not noticed them before, but Nicky didn't think that was it. She was an observant person; she would surely have noticed them before now.

Within the next few days, Nicky decided that the birds must have some sort of mysterious grapevine of their own, and word was getting round about the garden feasts. Her list of twelve different species had grown to more than twenty. There were greenfinches, bullfinches, siskins, mistle thrushes, pigeons, doves – even a couple of seagulls (heaven alone knew where they came from; they were miles from the sea). And on Wednesday, to everyone's surprise, a pair of jays flew in from the woods on the far side of the fields.

The only snag was that, with so many to eat

it, by the time Nicky came home from school on Wednesday afternoon the bag of food was almost gone.

"I'll get you another one, like I promised," Mum said. "But I'm not going into town till Friday, so they might have to do without for a day."

Nicky nodded. The birds certainly wouldn't starve in the meantime; in fact, she thought, it would probably do them good to have a day off. With an hour's daylight left, she put the very last of the food out on the lawn, turning the bag upside-down and shaking it while the sparrows and starlings watched, lined up on the gutter and phone wires and twittering to each other. They swooped almost before she was back in the house, and once again the lawn was covered with hopping, fluttering little bodies as the banquet disappeared.

On Thursday morning, the sparrows were cheeping outside Nicky's window again. They were starting to make a habit of this – it was going to get a bit annoying at the weekend, when she wanted a lie-in – and Nicky grinned wryly as she got out of bed.

"You're out of luck today," she said as she opened the curtains. "No more till tomorrow, so you'll just have to be patient."

There was a moment's silence. One particularly perky and acrobatic sparrow clung to the gutter edge and turned himself almost upside-down to look in at her. He chirped, as if he understood. Then the twittering started up again.

Downstairs, Pete said he had a cold coming on and thought he'd better not go to school. Mum looked at him sternly and said she couldn't see any sign of it and if he hadn't done his homework that was just bad luck. Hiding a grin, Nicky ate toast and peanut butter, and saved the crusts. At least she could give the birds something, to let them know she hadn't forgotten them.

It was colder than ever this morning. Leaving the house, Nicky shuddered at the bitter air, hunched into her coat and shoved her gloved hands deep into her pockets. "Come on!" she called to Pete, who was trailing disconsolately behind her. "We'd better jog to the bus stop, or we'll freeze solid on the way."

Pete didn't answer, but, from the hedge, something else did. It was a peculiar noise, half a whistle and half a raucous squawk, and it made her jump. Then she saw the starlings. There were at least twenty of them, huddled among the branches. They all seemed to be looking at her.

Then a second one whistled. It sounded like a querulous question, and Nicky grinned.

"Bad luck," she said. "I told the sparrows; there isn't any more till tomorrow."

Pete looked at her as if she'd just landed from outer space. "*Talking* to them now?" he said, and twirled a finger over his own head. "Nuts. Totally nuts!" He glowered at the starlings, then flapped his hands. "Go on, stupid birds; go away!"

The starlings didn't. They just sat there. Still looking at Nicky.

"Don't be so mean, Pete," Nicky admonished. "It's so cold, I don't suppose they feel like flying. Leave them alone."

Pete shrugged. The starlings continued to watch. And now Nicky noticed that the sparrows were arriving, too: a little army of them fluttering and jostling for position in the hedge. There was a lot of twittering, a few indignant cheeps, then they settled down, looking hopefully at her.

She had the toast crusts in her pocket, so she crumbled them and scattered them on the ground. A few of the birds flew down to investigate, but they only pecked at the crusts, discovered what they were, and went back to the hedge.

"Not impressed," said Pete. "They're getting picky."

"Go on," Nicky encouraged the birds. "Crusts are lovely; eat them up."

Pete rolled his eyes heavenwards. "Come on! Standing around here – you're the one who was moaning about the cold!"

She followed her brother out of the gate and away down the lane. Once or twice she looked back. The birds were still there in the hedge, and they'd been joined by two thrushes, a robin, a blackbird and a pigeon. Nicky felt a momentary twinge of guilt … and a twinge of unease, though she couldn't explain why. Then Pete called, "Come *on!*" again, and she turned and ran after him.

The birds were waiting when Nicky and Pete got home that afternoon.

This time, they weren't just in the hedge. There were sparrows and pigeons on the roof, starlings on the phone wire, finches on the electric wires. In fact there were birds everywhere.

And as soon as Nicky appeared, they all started twittering and chirping and squawking.

"What a din!" Pete covered his ears. "Shut up, you dumb birds! Shut up!"

This time the birds – or the nearest ones, anyway – did fly off when he windmilled his arms at them. But they didn't go very far.

"Poor things!" Nicky said compassionately. "They must be so hungry!"

"Hungry, my foot!" Pete snorted. "They've been eating themselves stupid for days. They're just plain *greedy.*" Then he paused. They were standing at the gate, looking over into the garden. A few of the more adventurous birds – mostly quite big ones – had landed on the grass and were doing a sort of inching, sideways waddle towards them, as though they were trying to get closer while pretending not to. "You know what this reminds me of?" said Pete. His voice sounded just the tiniest bit edgy.

"No," said Nicky. She was faintly edgy, too, but she didn't want to admit it even to herself.

"That Hitchcock film, *The Birds*," said Pete. "Remember? All these birds start gathering at this house, and—"

"I know, I've seen it!" Nicky snapped.

"Well, then. It's just like that, isn't it?"

"Course it isn't! The birds in the film attacked people!"

"Yeah. So what's going to happen when we open the gate and start walking up the path?"

He was just trying to wind her up, she was

sure of it. But there *was* something slightly menacing about the way the birds had gathered. The way they just sat there, staring. The twittering had subsided back into silence, and Nicky could almost feel a sense of hopefulness in the air. A sort of "Come on, where's our grub?" It was *creepy*.

Then suddenly common sense came back with a bang, and with it a surge of anger.

"You," she said to Pete, "are a pain!" And she flung the gate open and stalked up the path.

The birds didn't attack her. Of course they didn't; she'd known they wouldn't, and the whole Hitchcock thing was just her brother's prattish idea of a joke. All the same, by the time she reached the front door she was almost – though not quite – running.

And Pete was right on her heels.

They found Mum in the kitchen. She was putting a load of clothes into the washing machine, and she didn't look too pleased.

"Those wretched birds!" she grumbled. "I put some washing out – well, it's windy enough to dry it – and you know what? They all came and perched on the line. Knocked the pegs off, so half the stuff fell on the ground and got dirty again, and as for the rest of it..." She held out

Pete's dark blue shirt. There were yukky white smears all down the front.

"Oh, great!" said Pete. "Just what I've always wanted; a shirt covered in bird s—"

"All right, there's no need to point out the obvious!" Mum snapped. "And that's not all. While I was picking the clothes up again, something scored a direct hit on me! I'd only just washed my hair, and I had to go and do it all over again!"

Pete smothered a snigger, but Mum wasn't in the mood to laugh. "It's all your fault, Nicky," she went on. "Feeding them's fair enough, but you've really overdone it."

"Sorry, Mum," said Nicky. "I didn't think they'd be that hungry."

"Well, you'll just have to ration them in future."

Nicky nodded. "Did you give them anything today?"

Mum sighed, relenting. "I found some bread that was going stale. Not that they were very interested in it. And before you ask, yes, I *will* get another bag of that stuff tomorrow. But it'll be the last one."

Nicky nodded again. "OK. Thanks, Mum."

There was a sudden blur at the kitchen window, and a small thump.

"What was that?" Mum spun round.

Pete was staring at the window. "A bird," he said. "It flew straight at the window, as if it was trying to get in."

Nicky ran to look. "There's nothing there now."

"No. It flew away again." The edge was back in Pete's voice. "But there's *loads* of them outside on the grass."

"Can I give them something, Mum?" Nicky asked. "Please?"

"Ohh ... I suppose so. A few scraps or whatever. But not too much, all right?"

"All right. Thanks."

When she went outside with a bowl of bits scrounged from cupboards and the breadbin, Nicky was suddenly surrounded by birds. They fluttered down from every direction, chirping and hopping around her, all eager for food. When they found out what the food was, though, she could almost *feel* their reaction. They didn't want this stuff. It wasn't good enough. They were disappointed.

And a little bit annoyed.

Tap, tap.

"Mmmmpf..." muttered Nicky in her sleep.

Tap. Tap-tap-tap.

"Wha...?" Her brain crawled up to consciousness and she opened her eyes. What was that noise?

Tappity-tap. TaptaptaptaptapTAP!

Sounded like someone hammering a long way off. Yawning, and thoroughly annoyed at being woken so early, Nicky started to sit up in bed.

Chirrup.

It came from right outside her window. Those sparrows again. They must be—

KA-AK!

She jumped, her heart giving a wallopingly startled thump. That wasn't a sparrow! What on earth was going *on?*

Tappity-tappity-TAP! Chirp. Twitter. KA-AAK!

Nicky ran to the window, flung the curtains back – and there they were. Not just ranged along the gutter but actually sitting on the window sill. A row of faces with bright eyes and little beaks, looking in at her. Sparrows, robins, blackbirds, bluetits. And a magpie. Nicky's jaw dropped. She'd never seen anything like it – these birds were completely fearless! Stunned, she looked at the magpie. As soon as it saw her looking, its head went back, jabbed forward –

Tappity-tap! It was knocking on the window with its beak, and as if that was a signal, all the

103

other birds on the sill started doing the same.

Tap-TAPPY, tap-TAPPY, tap-TAPPY! Eerily, unnervingly, they were all pecking the glass in rhythm together. And to Nicky's rioting imagination the rhythm was like words. *Where IS it, where IS it, where IS it?* They were demanding their food. They wanted it, and they wanted it *now*.

Nicky yanked the curtains together again. But though she could shut out the sight of the birds, she couldn't shut out the sounds. *Tap-TAPPY, tap-TAPPY, tap-TAPPY!* It was like drums; it wouldn't stop! Her heart was pounding like a hammer under her ribs now, and suddenly her nerve snapped and she shouted, "Stop it! Be quiet! Go *away!*"

"Nicks?" It was Pete's voice, outside her door. He came in, stopped, listened for a moment, then said in a hollow, scared voice, "Oh, no... Not you, too?"

"Th-they're outside your window?" said Nicky.

He nodded. "Hundreds of them. They woke me up. You've really started something, haven't you?"

"Don't!" she pleaded. "It's scary, Pete – it's as if they're ganging up on us!"

"Just like the Hitchcock film; I told you."

Nicky shivered, not wanting to think about that. "What about Mum and Dad?" she asked. "Do they know?"

Pete was about to say, "I think they're still asleep," but before he could speak, a bleary voice across the landing said crossly, "What on earth is going *on*?"

Mum appeared, in her dressing-gown. "What's all that noise?" she demanded. "If you two have woken me up at this uncivilized hour—"

"It isn't us, Mum." Nicky went to the window and lifted the curtain back, just enough for a cluster of small, feathery faces to be visible. "It's *them*."

"What? *Ohh!* Those *blasted* birds!" Unlike Nicky and Pete, though, Mum wasn't unnerved; she was simply annoyed. "I tell you, Nicky, this is getting beyond a joke, and it's got to stop! If it wasn't for the fact that I'd promised to get some more of that food—"

"Please, Mum, don't say you won't!" Nicky begged.

"I didn't say that. I promised, so I will. But after that, no more!" Mum sighed grumpily. "Well, there's no point trying to get back to sleep, so I might as well go downstairs and put the kettle on." She turned to go, then paused.

"Why you're still feeling sorry for the little wretches when they're making such nuisances of themselves is beyond me!"

Nicky didn't answer. The truth was, Mum had misinterpreted the reason why she was pleading for another bag of food. She wasn't feeling sorry for the birds any more.

She was getting *scared* of them.

The birds kept it up all through breakfast. They sat on the window sills, they tapped at the glass, they fluttered against the panes, beating with their wings to attract attention. Their shadows flickered and danced across the kitchen, and by the time breakfast was over, everyone's nerves were jangling.

Nicky got ready for school amid a background chorus of cheeping and tapping at her window. As she started back downstairs, she heard Pete's voice in the hall.

"I'm *sure* I've got a cold coming on, Mum! Can't I—"

"No!" came Mum's sharp reply. "You're going to school, and that's that! Ah, Nicky – there you are at last. Hurry up, the pair of you, or you'll miss the bus!"

She stomped to the kitchen to load the dishwasher. Pete and Nicky looked at the front door. Then they looked at each other.

"Got to do it," Nicky said.

"Yeah..." said Pete in a small voice.

"Right then; together. One – two – three!"

They jerked the front door open, and ran down the path.

Quite what she'd expected to happen, Nicky didn't know. Maybe she'd thought they would be dive-bombed by a whole squadron of everything from finches to golden eagles, plummeting out of the sky and zooming at them like jet fighters. Or maybe she'd thought they would wade into a sea of hopping, feathery bodies, all chirping, *"Where IS it, where IS it, where IS it?"*

She and Pete piled through the gate, almost getting stuck as they both tried to be first, and they were out in the lane before it dawned on them that nothing *had* happened. Nothing at all.

Except for a sinister feeling of being *watched*.

Slowly, they turned and looked back at the garden.

The birds were there. Pete was right; there were hundreds of them now. Just about every space large enough to perch on was covered with them. And all over the grass, the hedge, even down the house's brick walls, was ... well, it looked as if it had been snowing.

"Mum's going to go *berserk* when she sees that mess," Pete whispered.

Nicky swallowed. "I think," she said, "that's the least of our worries..."

A sparrow, sitting on the top of the hedge, uttered an inquiring *cheep*? Nicky and Pete looked at each other again. Then: "Run!" hissed Pete.

They pelted towards the bus stop.

"I only hope Mum's remembered," Nicky said as they climbed off the school bus that afternoon and started to walk towards their house.

Pete hunched his shoulders. "Somehow, I don't think she'll have been allowed to forget."

It had been an awful day at school. Neither of them could concentrate on anything; and at break, Nicky had been half terrified to venture out to the playground. She had the horrible feeling that the birds might have come after her, and would be lined up on the school roof, waiting. They weren't. But the sight of a blackbird hopping along the top of a wall had been enough to send her scurrying indoors again.

"Come on," Pete said, breaking in on her gloomy thoughts. "Better find out the worst."

They quickened their steps, and both took a

deep breath before they turned into the lane. The lane curved and the hedges on either side were pretty high, so it wasn't possible to see their own house until they were right on top of it. They reached the gate. And there...

Nicky stopped, baffled. There wasn't a bird in sight. Not a single one.

"Oh..." she said.

Pete was staring in astonishment, too. "Where've they all gone?"

They ran up the path. The yukky mess of bird-lime was still smeared on everything, but the birds themselves weren't there. Not so much as a chirp broke the quiet.

Pete put his key in the front door. "Mum?" he called as they went in.

Mum appeared from the living-room, and they bombarded her with questions.

"Mum, where are all the birds?"

"What's happened outside?"

"Did you go to town?"

"Did you get the—"

"Yes, of course I did!" Mum snapped. She looked flustered, Nicky noticed suddenly. Very flustered. And more than a little wild-eyed.

"Then where are all the birds?" Pete persisted. "There aren't any out the front."

"Aren't there?" Mum snarled. "Then go and look at the back garden!"

They ran through to the kitchen and peered out of the window.

"Good grief!" said Nicky.

The lawn was *covered* with birds. So many of them that you could hardly see the grass. They were all happily pecking, and in between them it was just possible to make out the garish colours of the bird food.

"It's been like that all afternoon," said Mum, coming in. "And as soon as they've finished one lot, they start flapping round the house and banging on the windows again, until they get more." She pointed to the table. "Look how much they've eaten already!"

Nicky looked, and her eyes widened. Nearly a quarter of the new bag was gone.

"Like I said this morning," Mum went on, "when they finish this, they are *not* going to get any more. It's ridiculous – we'll go bankrupt at this rate!"

A large rook looked towards the window. It cocked its head on one side, as if it was thinking about something, then it made a shuffling, sidelong hop towards the house.

"Looks as if that latest helping's almost gone," said Mum.

"Can I put some more out?" Nicky asked.

But Mum had had enough. "No," she said, "you can't. It'll be dark soon and they'll all go wherever birds go at night. Leave it till the morning."

"But—"

"I said, *no*." Mum grabbed the bag and shoved it away in a cupboard. "They're going to have to learn to do without, so they might as well start now."

Nicky looked out of the window again. The rook had sidled closer, and so had several starlings. They looked hopeful. They looked hungry.

They looked *impatient*.

"I wish we had a cat," said Pete as he and Nicky crept downstairs at dawn the next morning.

"So do I," she agreed. "Preferably several."

"Or best of all, a Siberian tiger. God, just *listen* to the noise they're making!"

Any hopes of a Saturday lie-in had been squashed flat. As soon as the first glimmer of light appeared in the sky, the birds had started, chirruping and squawking and pecking at the bedroom windows. Mum, livid, had told Pete and Nicky to get downstairs and "Do something about it!" and so here they were, hurrying to satisfy the voracious appetites of their garden visitors.

"I know why they're called wildlife now," Pete commented sourly as they padded into the kitchen. "They're driving me wild, all right."

Something thumped against the window, and something else against the door, as Nicky went to fetch the bag of bird food. "It's a pity the lady I talked to wasn't in the shop when Mum went in yesterday," she said. "She might have known what to do."

Mum hadn't been impressed by the shop, she'd told them. It fact it had given her the creeps: poky, grotty and full of dark, gloomy corners. She couldn't imagine what had possessed Nicky to go in there in the first place. And the only sales assistant she'd seen was a sullen and surly boy who didn't know anything about anything, and didn't care either. Still, there was plenty of the garish food left. So when this lot ran out – and Nicky was starting to wonder if it would last the weekend – then if the worst came to the worst she could get some more with her own money.

"Right, I've got it." She lugged the bag across the floor. "Open the back door."

The noise outside rose to new volumes as Pete cautiously eased the door open. Nicky had to brace herself to step outside – but as soon as the birds saw the bag in her hand, absolute silence fell.

"Hurry up!" Pete urged from the doorway.

Nicky grabbed handfuls of food and scattered it over the grass. The birds didn't waste a moment. They weren't the least bit afraid of her now, and they swooped in a single huge mass of wings.

"*Look out!*" Pete shouted, and Nicky ducked just in time as an enormous crow hurtled past her head. With a squeal she pelted for the back door, and a seagull dived seemingly from nowhere. It missed her by a hair's breadth, and as it skimmed past it turned its head and its beak lunged at the bag.

"Nicky, it's coming back! *Run!*" Pete yelled. The gull wheeled, plummeted –

"*No-oo!*" Nicky shrieked. She made it into the kitchen centimetres ahead of the gull, and Pete slammed the door as the bird rocketed towards it. There was a loud thump, a furious squawk, and the gull staggered dizzily away, ruffling its wings.

"Oh my God, that was close!" Nicky gasped, leaning against the table.

"Tell me about it," Pete said. "Nicks, this is getting *dangerous*! That stuff's done something awful to the birds! We *mustn't* give them any more of it!"

She nodded, still trying to get her breath. "Yeah. You're right. I'll explain to Mum and Dad. We'll have to put up with all the squawking for a day or two, but it should wear off after that."

"Yeah," said Pete. "It should. Shouldn't it...?"

"It's no good." Nicky clenched her fists in an effort to stop herself from shaking. "I know what we all agreed. But I've *got* to, Pete. I've got to feed them!"

"You can't!" Pete protested. "It'll only make things worse!"

"I know that! But I can't stand this any more!"

The birds were getting angry – and Nicky was getting scared. Because angry birds were a very, very different proposition from the dear, harmless little Feathered Friends that everyone knew and loved. When the food stopped appearing, it hadn't taken them long to realize what was going on. And when they did, they had their own ways of showing their annoyance.

You only had to look at a window, and there they were. Lined up. Staring in. *Waiting.* They goggled into the kitchen, the living-room, the dining-room, the bedrooms. Even through the frosted bathroom window you could see their blurry shapes.

The birds were *everywhere*. No one could open a door without at least ten of them trying to hop into the house. No one dared open a window, because they'd be through it like a shot. As the day went on the numbers grew and grew, until by lunchtime they were blocking half the light out of every room and Mum had to switch all the lamps on.

Nicky and Pete had tried going outside. Once. And they'd both come back shuddering, with a silent, reproachful trail of birds hopping behind them. Pete had a huge dollop of bird-lime in his hair and Nicky had two on her shoulders. But no one was laughing. It was simply not funny any more.

Now, just when Nicky had shut herself in her room, drawn the curtains and tried to settle down to watch a video, the noise had started again. Ten times louder than ever before.

"It's no good!" she said again. "I've got to feed them, Pete, or I'll go completely crazy! I'm going to talk to Mum!"

Mum agreed without any argument that the birds could be fed again, and Nicky realized with an inward shiver that she and Dad were as nervous as she was. The birds were delighted.

Oh, they were *delighted*. Nicky hurled down four enormous handfuls of food, then scuttled back to the sanctuary of the house with a storm of flying shapes diving and swooping around her. Down to the lawn came birds in their hundreds, pecking, flapping, vying for the choicest bits. This time, the food lasted no more than ten minutes. And then they were back at the windows.

Three more times they fed the birds before the sun went down. Three more times the food vanished almost as soon as it was put down.

And the birds queued up at the windows again.

After tea, Mum called an emergency family meeting. It was completely dark now, and in theory the birds should have gone. But Nicky and Pete both thought they could still hear chirping outside. No one was willing to open the curtains and look, though. Just in case.

"Right," said Mum as they all sat down. "I don't know what's in that bird food, but it must be something pretty horrific. They're completely hooked on it!"

"Like Nicky and chocolate biscuits," Dad put in, valiantly trying to make a joke. But no one even smiled.

"So I've been thinking," Mum continued.

"When I was a kid, we had this cat called Miggins. She got mad keen on a particular brand of cat food, and she refused to eat anything else. It was really expensive stuff and we couldn't afford it. So we weaned her off it slowly. We started mixing it with cheaper food, a bit at a time. Then we gradually increased the amount of the cheaper stuff, until Miggins got the message. It took a while, but it worked."

"So you reckon we could do it with the birds?" Nicky asked.

"If it worked with her, it should work with them. Cats are much fussier."

"It's worth a try," said Dad. "*Anything's* worth a try."

"OK. Then we'll start tomorrow." Mum looked relieved. She stood up –

Chirrup!

It came from the window sill. It definitely did.

As if something had heard, and understood.

At first, they thought the experiment was going to work. The birds were waiting as usual next morning, and the instant the back door opened, they came hurtling to get their breakfast. Nicky and Pete watched from the window while everything was devoured, then as the birds finished the last scraps and headed for the window sill again, they backed away and returned to the kitchen.

"Your turn first," said Nicky. The second batch of food was ready and waiting, and whoever put it out was to check and see if any of the first lot had been left.

Pete gulped. "OK. Here goes!"

He did it at a run, pausing only to look hard at the lawn. As he rushed back inside, Nicky demanded, "Well?"

"They've eaten everything," Pete said.

"Are you sure?"

"Certain. There isn't a single bit of anything left."

"Brilliant! Then let's hope this keeps them quiet for a bit."

It didn't. The food was gone in ten minutes, and the birds were back. Though the noise got on her nerves, Nicky made them wait half an hour before she served breakfast number three. Again, it looked like they'd eaten every scrap. But as she raced back to the house with a skyful of birds swooping around her, Nicky saw a small heap of cake crumbs lying in the middle of the lawn.

And that was the start of it.

The birds were clever, all right. By lunchtime, they'd learned to separate the things they did want from the things they didn't. The grass was littered with crumbs, crusts – all the stuff that had been so carefully mixed with the garish food to fool them. It wasn't fooling them, not any more.

And the moment a new batch of food was finished, they were back. Crowding at the windows. Waiting outside the doors.

By dusk, almost all the new bag's contents had been eaten. And when darkness fell, the birds didn't go away. There was no doubting it this time; Dad had looked outside, and what he saw made him hastily shut the curtains again. When he turned round, his face was white.

"Linda," he said to Mum, "I think maybe we'd better phone the police."

"Police?" Nicky and Pete were aghast.

"Or the fire brigade – I don't know; somebody who can do something. They're besieging us."

For several seconds there was an awful silence. Then, from outside, they all heard a clear: *KA-AK*.

Mum's mouth set into a tight line and she made for the phone.

"Hello? Yes, police, please. Yes; I'm ringing from Bemleigh. Three-one-double-oh-six. Thank you."

They all hovered, listening, while Mum waited to get through to the police station. Nicky was *sure* she could hear the birds twittering outside, like a conference. Then: "Hello, police? This is going to sound very strange, but it's the birds in our garden. They've suddenly... Hello? Hello, are you still there? *Hello?*"

"What is it?" Dad hissed.

Mum looked round slowly. "The line's gone dead."

"What?" Dad grabbed the phone, banged it, rattled the receiver rest, banged it again.

"Nothing," he said. "I can't even get the dialling tone. We've been cut off!"

It didn't take a genius to guess what had happened. The birds. They must have pecked or pulled the outside cable away from its connector.

They must have *known*.

"Mum, you gave the operator our number," Nicky said desperately. "Maybe the police'll come here anyway."

But Mum shook her head. "I only got as far as saying it was something to do with birds. They won't turn out for that. They probably think it was a crank call."

From the garden came a soft, low twittering. It sounded almost like laughter.

Dad looked round the room uneasily. "We can't phone anyone, and trying to go outside in the dark would be very stupid," he said. "I think the best thing we can do is make sure all the doors and windows are locked, and go to bed."

"I won't sleep a wink!" Mum protested.

"I don't suppose any of us will. But at least when it gets light we can see what's going on. Nicky, save the last of that bird food till morning. We might need it."

They did try to sleep. But no one succeeded, and as soon as it began to get light, they were all downstairs again.

The birds were there. If you'd asked her to guess, Nicky would have said there were thousands of them by now, and they completely blocked the light from the windows.

"Why haven't the neighbours done something?" Nicky asked nervously. "They must have noticed!"

"Don't be so sure," said Dad. "We're almost at the end of the lane, remember; there's only old Mrs Thompson beyond us, and she's nearly blind. So how many people ever see our house?"

Pete said, "I don't want to go to school."

For once, he wasn't trying to find an excuse. All the same, though, Mum shook her head. "I think you'd better," she said. "Both of you. It's safer. Look, I've got an idea." She looked at Dad. "When you get to work, Frank, call out the phone company to fix our line. Then ring the police." She shivered. "Or if they won't come, just get *someone*. I'll stay here, and—"

"I don't think you should!" Dad protested. "Come to town with me, in the car."

Mum shook her head. "Someone's got to be here for the phone engineers. Anyway..." She glanced nervously towards the window. "I've got a feeling that if the birds see us all leaving, they might turn *really* nasty, and do something to stop us going. If there's one person still in the house, the rest of you should be able to get away."

No one liked Mum's idea one bit, but no one could come up with anything better. There was enough food left – just – to distract the birds while Dad, Nicky and Pete got out of the house, so they all made a big show of following the normal morning routine. Dad drove away in the car, Nicky and Pete headed for the bus stop, and Mum waved them off then firmly shut the front door.

All through the long morning at school, Nicky couldn't stop worrying. And one thing in particular was bugging her badly. By lunchtime she was nearly exploding with it, and when she was able to talk to Pete, she discovered that he had been thinking along the same lines.

"What if Dad *can't* get anyone to go to the house?" Pete said worriedly. "Mum's going to be on her own all day. And there's hardly any of that food left..."

"I know. I'm scared, Pete. Scared for Mum."

"Me, too." Pete was silent for a few moments. Then: "How much money have you got on you?" he asked.

They'd had their allowances at the weekend. "About four quid," said Nicky.

"I've got three-fifty. Nicks, do you reckon we should...?"

"Go into town and get another bag?"

"Yeah. Just in case..."

Another silence. Then Nicky nodded. "Yes. I think we should." She looked surreptitiously around to see if there were any teachers in sight, and lowered her voice. "And I don't think we should wait till after school."

Pete glanced around, too. The coast was clear...

"There's a bus to town in about five minutes. Come on, before anyone sees us..."

The bus dropped them outside the cinema, and they hurried along the high street towards the side road where the pet shop was.

Or where it had been.

"No!" said Nicky, aghast. "Oh, *no!*"

The shop itself was still there, of course. But where the window had been full of food and toys and baskets and all sorts of other petty paraphernalia, now it was completely empty. Except for a piece of paper Sellotaped forlornly in the middle of the glass.

The paper read simply:

GONE AWAY

"I don't *believe* it!" Pete stared through the window to the blank, bare shop interior. There wasn't so much as a flea-comb in there. Every last scrap of stock had vanished as surely as if it had been spirited away.

"Pete," Nicky said in a small voice, "where's the nearest phone box...?"

They found one, and Pete dialled their own number. He listened for a few moments, then replaced the receiver. His face was pale, and he said, "It's the Number Unobtainable tone..."

Then the phone engineers hadn't got to the house yet. Were the police there? Or was Mum still waiting? Nicky thought of her alone in the house. Alone with the birds...

Pete saw her face and knew what she was thinking. School was completely forgotten. "There isn't a bus back for half an hour..." he said.

Nicky swallowed. "We can't wait that long. Can we?"

Pete hesitated, but only for half a second. Then he said, "No!"

They turned away from the locked and deserted shop, and they started to run.

Nicky and Pete raced up the lane – and stopped dead as they saw the two cars. One was Dad's. It was slewed sideways across the lane, with its nose buried in the hedge and one front wing crumpled. The driver's door hung open, sagging on its hinges, but Dad wasn't anywhere to be seen.

The other car was a police panda. It was parked at an angle, as if it had arrived and stopped in a heck of a hurry, but like Dad's there was no one inside it.

In fact there was no sign of anyone at all.

Nicky's heart began to pound and she felt sick. She couldn't bring herself to even look at Pete; instead she started to run again, racing towards their house. The high hedge obscured it; then she reached the gate and suddenly the house was visible.

Nicky skidded to a halt again, and Pete collided with her. Together, they stared.

There was the house. The broken phone wire

still dangled, and the walls were still streaked with white. But the birds…

The birds had gone. There wasn't a single one anywhere.

"Where are they?" Nicky whispered.

Pete swallowed. "Where's *anyone*?"

Raising her voice, Nicky called, "Hello? Is anybody there?"

No answer. Nicky called again. Still nothing.

Pete eased the gate open, peering cautiously from side to side as if he expected something to hurl itself at him out of the hedge. Nothing did. The gate creaked, tapped back against the post, and he and Nicky started to tiptoe up the path.

They were half-way along it, with still no sign of a single, solitary bird, when suddenly and violently the front door banged open. They both yelped with shock, jumping and clutching at each other – then froze as they saw the figures who came stumbling out into the garden.

"*Mum?*" Pete's voice went up in a squeak of sheer disbelief.

It *was* Mum – but her hair was a wild tangle and her clothes were torn and ripped. She hadn't got any shoes on, and there were livid red scratch-marks all over her arms and legs and face. A policewoman was helping her. She saw Nicky and Pete and said sharply, "You children, go back outside the gate!" They didn't move, and she added more kindly, "It's all right, there's nothing to be frightened of. Your mum and dad have had a bit of trouble, but it's going to be all right."

Nicky ran to Mum and hugged her, and Pete said in a quavering voice, "Where's Dad? What's *happened*?"

"Your dad's in the house. Don't worry; he's OK, but – Hey!" as Nicky and Pete dived towards the door. "Where are you going? Come back!"

But she was too involved with helping Mum to grab them as they dashed past her and piled through the door.

Slid to a halt.

Froze.

Stared, with open mouths and goggling eyes.

Nicky found her voice first, though it came out as a tiny, thin squeak. "What on earth—?"

Pete swallowed. He couldn't say a word: the whole scene was just too unspeakably mad.

Then their paralysis broke and they started to run from room to room.

Every one was a total wreck. Furniture lay overturned, cushions had been torn to pieces, pictures and ornaments and even the TV screen were smashed to smithereens. There were huge gouges and scratches everywhere: on tables, on the walls, on the ceiling. The kitchen looked as if a tornado had ripped through it. Every single window was broken – and every surface was streaked and smeared with white stains of bird lime.

The truth started to dawn on Nicky, but before she could say anything a familiar voice called from above them. "Pete? Nicky? Is that you?"

"It's Dad!" Pete shouted. They pelted back to the hall, and met Dad coming down the stairs, with a policeman behind him. He wasn't as dishevelled as Mum, but he looked every bit as shocked.

"Don't go up there," he said, holding out a warning hand.

Nicky's eyes were wide. "They trashed upstairs, too?"

Dad nodded grimly. "Everything."

"How did they get in?" Pete asked.

"They made a mass attack on the windows, your mum says," the policeman told them. "Broke the lot."

Dad, it seemed, had got back in the middle of it all. He could hardly see the house for a heaving, fluttering mass of birds, and he was so shocked that he crunched the car. He'd tried to battle his way inside, but the birds beat him back.

Then the police car swung into the lane. The driver had seen the chaos, started the siren up – and the birds scattered. The multitude outside the house flew away as if a squadron of eagles was after them, and as the policeman and policewoman scrambled to help Dad, all the birds inside came hurtling out through the windows in a squawking, flapping tidal wave of feathers. In less than two minutes, every single one had vanished.

"It was like something out of a horror film," the policeman said. "If I hadn't seen it for myself, I'd never have believed it!" He managed a smile at Nicky and Pete. "But it's all over now, and your mum and dad are both all right, even if the house isn't." He looked at Dad. "Right then, sir. If you're feeling up to it, we'll take your wife to hospital for a checkover, then go down to the station and get this on record."

Soberly, they all left the house. Outside, Nicky and Pete peered nervously around, but there wasn't a bird to be seen. Not a single, solitary one.

Mum was in the back of the police car, with a rug round her shoulders. The policewoman was talking to her, and she looked a bit calmer. At the gate, Dad paused. Then he said, "Officer ... when we get to the station, can I make a phone call?" The policeman said of course he could, and Nicky frowned. "Who do you want to call, Dad?"

"The local estate agent," Dad told her. He looked back at the house. He frowned. "I'm going to put the house on the market, right *now*. Whatever else happens, we're not going back there again!"

"Never...?" ventured Pete.

Slowly and determinedly, Dad shook his head. "Never, ever, *ever*."

Pussycat, Pussycat, Where Have You Been?

Everyone's gone to bed now. It's Christmas Day tomorrow; Mum's tired, Dad's grumpy, and the little kids are excited. They've hung up their stockings, ready for Santa, and they'll wake up far too early and drive everyone mad.

The sitting-room looks very festive. There's the tree, standing in the window so that anyone going past can see it. The tree lights flash different colours, which Mum likes but Dad thinks is naff. But he doesn't dare to argue with her. The tree lights are switched off now, though. All the lights in the house are switched off.

There are Christmas cards on the sideboard and the mantelpiece, and more, pinned to strips of red ribbon, hanging on the walls. The family who live here have had a lot of Christmas cards this year. There are all sorts of different pictures, mostly of animals or birds. Funny, isn't it, how many Christmas cards have creatures on them? You could count eight reindeer (three with red noses), five lots of horses pulling jolly Victorian coaches through the snow, ten dear little puppies or kittens sitting by the fire, six penguins, three mice, two hedgehogs, and fifteen robins. There's a kookaburra, too. That's from Cousin Jane in Australia, where the wildlife's different and Christmas tends to be very hot. And the next-door neighbours have sent a Diwali card, with beautiful, exotic birds of paradise in jewel colours.

There's also a card with a cross-eyed cartoon rabbit on it, surrounded by chocolate eggs. Inside, it says, "Happy Easter". That one's from Great-Great-Uncle Vic. Uncle Vic's very old and extremely eccentric, and he tends to get things mixed up. Still, it's the thought that counts.

Oh, and there's one other card. It's on the sideboard, pushed a bit behind the others. It's got confusing swirly patterns round the edge, and in the middle is a picture of a black cat. But not a friendly, homely, purry cat like the ones on other cards. This one's ears are flattened against its head, and its eyes are narrowed to furious, emerald-green slits. Its mouth is open in a threatening snarl. It's a cat with *attitude*.

No one's quite sure who sent this card. There was an ordinary stamp on the envelope, but the postmark was too smudged to read. And all that's written in it is: "Season's Greetings To You All". No name, and no one recognizes the handwriting.

Dad took one look at the card and said it must be from that weirdo arty woman Mum goes to Keep Fit with. Maybe it is. Or maybe it's from one of the kids' school mates, who wanted to be different. Whatever the truth, there's something about that card that gives everyone the creeps. I mean, it's not exactly Christmassy, is it? Season of Goodwill, and all that. A snarling cat, looking as if if can't wait to claw your eyes out. Oh, thanks a bunch!

But it's only a card, isn't it? And it's tucked away so that it doesn't show. Much better to look at the robins and horses and reindeer and dear little puppies. Even the cross-eyed rabbit. At least he's fun.

Anyway, Christmas Eve. It isn't snowing, but never mind. There's snow on the cards, and spray-on snow on the tree, so everyone can pretend. It's getting late now. The clock on the wall says five to twelve. Almost midnight, and

135

then it'll be Christmas Day. A car goes past in the road, and for a moment the headlamps shine through the curtains and light up the sitting room. Then everything's still and quiet again.

A breathless sort of stillness. A *waiting* sort of quietness.

Then, far away in the distance, a church clock starts to strike. *Bong. Bong. Bong.* It sounds very solemn. You can't help counting the chimes. Four ... five ... six ... seven...

Another flicker of light shivers through the room. But there's no car passing by now. Maybe it was just imagination?

Bong. Bong. Bong. That's ten.

Was that a shadow, in the corner of the room? Just for a moment, something seemed to *move*...

Bong. Bonggggg.

The last stroke of the clock dies slowly away into silence. It truly is midnight now.

And that shadow isn't imagination at all.

It's on the sideboard, at the back. It isn't terribly big, but it's definitely there. And it's moving. Slowly, slinkily, stealthily. It pauses. There's a tiny sound, like something sniffing. Then: "*Mrrowrr...*"

The family haven't got a cat.

Or have they? Because that small, sleek shape

picking its way so carefully among the Christmas cards has two pointed ears, four soft paws, and a long, slowly waving tail.

And emerald green eyes. Eyes that glow in the gloom with an eerie, inner light.

And the card at the back of the sideboard, the mystery one with the unknown sender, has changed. The swirling, coloured patterns round the border are still there.

But the middle of the picture is blank.

The shadow creeps on, then stops. The green eyes stare at one of the other cards, which shows jolly penguins in a scene of snow and icebergs.

"*Mrrowwr?*" It sounds like a question. And suddenly the shadow isn't there any more. Instead, a cold breath of air that could have come from the South Pole blows wintrily through the room. If you could see the penguin card properly in the darkness, you might notice a small, dark shape slinking across the ice, heading straight for a penguin with a woolly hat on.

There's a squawk, then a very catty sort of hiss. The wind stops, and next moment the shadow is back on the sideboard. It shakes itself. It sneezes. It licks a half-frozen paw. *Too cold!*

It moves on to the next card. This one has two

little mice, eating berries under a snowy tree. *Sweet* little mice. Ah, *that's* better...

The shadow vanishes again. The mouse card goes dark. There's a shrill squeak, then another. The shadow returns, and a pink tongue appears briefly, licking round its whiskers.

On the card, now, there's a snowy tree and some half-eaten berries. And two blank spaces.

There's a hedgehog on the next card, but as the shadow approaches it rolls itself into a prickly ball. The shadow hesitates, then prowls on. The hedgehog doesn't unroll itself.

On across the sideboard goes the dark shape, until it reaches Cousin Jane's kookaburra. *Interesting.* And suddenly the room becomes hot, as if the midsummer sun is beating down. There's a frenzied flapping, and then a raucous noise that seems to echo from a long, *long* way off: "*Uh-uh-oo-oo-oo-YARK-YARK-YARK!*"

"*MmmmrrrWOWR! Sssss!*"

The noises fade. The heat dies away. It's a very nice picture on Cousin Jane's card, but a bit boring. Eucalyptus trees and a couple of butterflies. That's all.

On again. But there's nothing else interesting on the sideboard; the rest of the cards are all Santas and dinky villages and abstract patterns. So with a movement like dark, flowing water, the shadow jumps down to the floor and glides across the carpet. On the wall hang two red ribbons, with more cards pinned to them. What have we here? Ah … *robins*. All fifteen of them. Someone thought they should all be displayed together. Now, wasn't *that* thoughtful?

The shadow looks at the dangling ends of the ribbons. They're not very far above its head. It stretches upwards, extending itself like a concertina. A slender paw reaches, claws bared.

Slash. Tug. Tug, tug…

Down comes the first ribbon.

Swipe. Tug.

The second ribbon flops to the floor.

Now there's a new sound. Twittering, agitated, panicky. Some of the cards start to flip and flutter where they lie. The shadow isn't in the room any more. One by one the cards go dark briefly, as if something *much* larger than robins is climbing into the pictures.

Then the flipping and fluttering stops. There's no more twittering, not any more. Strange, the Christmas cards some people choose. I mean, there's nothing to *look* at on these, is there?

It's very, very quiet now. Not a sound anywhere. Not a whisper of noise from the four black paws that pad towards the mantelpiece. The shadow stops again. Looks again. Very carefully, with green eyes that can see in the dark. Oh, yes. Oh, *yes*...

A leap, light as a feather, and it's up on the mantelpiece. It's much too clever and graceful to disturb anything. It knows *exactly* what it wants, and it moves resolutely towards it.

The Easter Bunny on Great-Great-Uncle Vic's card doesn't see a thing. It's cross-eyed, after all, so all it can look at is its own twitching nose.

Not for long, though. There's no shadow on the mantelpiece. There's a hideous, gruesome *crunching* noise, that goes on for a very long time.

"*Mrrrrr.*" It's a very contented sound, almost like purring. In the middle of the floor, a small black shape sits peacefully washing its paws, concentrating until they're perfectly clean. Then it stands up, stretches, looks around. Nothing else? No. Anyway, it's *very* full. And out there, beyond the room, there's a whole wide world, just waiting to be explored.

"*Mmmm.*"

The Christmas tree shakes slightly as something pushes past it to the window. A couple of the fairy lights slip off the branches and hang in mid-air. Then the curtain twitches briefly, and there's a funny little draught in the room. As if the window has somehow opened itself for a moment, then shut again.

It's well past midnight now. Christmas Day. Very, *very* still. Very, *very* quiet.

The clock in the distance is chiming six when the two little kids can't wait any more, and come thundering downstairs to see what Santa's brought them. They slam the light on.

And stop, staring. At the sideboard. The mantelpiece. The carpet.

The *carpet* – Oh, *yucch*!

The younger kid bursts into a storm of noisy tears, while the older one hurtles back into the hall and screams hysterically up the stairs.

"Mum, Dad, come *quick*! *MU-U-UM!!*"

Their parents don't even *look* at the cards with their blank spaces. They're too horrified by what's on the floor. Feathers. Lots of them; mostly brown but with a few brightly coloured ones mixed in. Tufts of rabbit fur.

And *blood*...

Both the little kids are howling now, and the older ones have come down, bleary-eyed, asking what all the racket's about. No one explains. No one *can* explain.

They do notice the cards, eventually. Some of them have got bloodstains on them, too. And as for that weird one, the one with the black cat...

141

When they pick it up, they could swear for a moment that they hear a sound of *purring*.

The older kids look at each other. They've both got the same theory. But no way are they going to share it with anyone else. I mean, it's too crazy, isn't it? Much, much too crazy. Things like that can't *happen*.

Mum takes the little ones back upstairs to comfort them, while Dad clears up the fur and feathers and starts trying to get the stains out of the carpet. The older kids help. Everyone's very quiet, because no one can think of a single thing to say.

And outside, in the garden, a small shape crouches under a holly bush. It's still dark, so even if you knew where to look you probably wouldn't see it. But it's there. Now and then, it licks its whiskers and gives a little purr. It's still feeling very full. But that won't last for ever. By the time evening comes, and the world's dark again, it'll be hungry.

So all it has to do is wait.

Season's Greetings, everyone.

From the brand-new member of your family...

Rudolph the
Red-Eyed Reindeer

When the phone in Dad's office started ringing at 8 p.m. on Christmas Eve, Mum groaned and said, "I knew it. It *had* to happen!"

Dad had just gone upstairs to run a bath, so Tony went through to the office and picked up the receiver.

"Hello – Belton's Breakdown Service. Can I help you?" he said in his most efficient voice.

The line crackled and fizzed so badly that it sounded as if the call was coming from Jupiter. All Tony could make out was a man's tinny and extremely agitated voice shouting something about: "... blasted thing (*fzzzz-splutter-WHEEP!*) ran out on me!"

"Sorry, I didn't get all of that!" Tony bawled back. The guy must be on a mobile, he thought;

145

with half a gale *and* a blizzard blowing it was a miracle he got through at all. "What happened?"

"(*Bllrrrrr*) – tree! – (*splutter-splutter-crack*) – crashed, didn't it? – (*shriek, POP!*) – get here as quick as you can!"

"Where are you?" Tony yelled.

"(*Fzzzzzzzz*) —orp Road! (*Mumble blah*) tee-junction – (*WHEEP!*) – thundering great oak tree, you can't miss it! Neither did I!"

Aha – got it! Tony knew the junction with the tree very well indeed. So did Dad. He got a lot of call-outs from there, specially when the roads were covered with snow and ice.

"OK!" he shouted down the phone. "Hang on, and we'll be with you in about twenty minutes! Oh – what sort of vehicle is it?"

"(*Blllrrrr*) —EH!"

"WHAT – SORT – OF – VEHICLE?"

"... just told you! A – (*vrrrrARP*) —eh!"

Oh hell, what did it matter? Some make of car ending in "eh", that must be it. "OK!" Tony bellowed again. "We're on our way!"

Mum had her long-suffering look on when he went back into the sitting-room. "I heard," she said. "I've shouted to Dad; he's coming down."

"Can I go with him, Mum?"

"Oh *Tony*! Not in this weather!"

"Please! There's no one else to help him, is

there?" To tell the truth, Tony was secretly delighted that this job had come up. He'd been bored stiff; there was nothing on TV and nothing else to do except hang around waiting for bed time. A bit of excitement was just what he needed.

"Oh ... all right, I suppose he can't do it all on his own," said Mum reluctantly. "But wrap up warm. It's *freezing* out there."

Five minutes later, the roar of a powerful engine shattered the quiet, and in a billowing fog of exhaust the pick-up truck trundled out of the small yard at the side of the house. Tony, in the passenger seat, peered through the driving snow as they turned right and started up the long hill. What a night! And when they got high up, on those twisty roads where the junction was, it was going to be even wilder. He felt sorry for the guy who'd phoned, crunching his car in weather like this. He'd probably be half frozen, which was why Mum had shoved a flask of hot coffee into Tony's hand as he was dashing out of the door.

He rubbed at the windscreen, which kept misting up because the truck's engine hadn't warmed up yet. Dad said, "Thanks," as his side was cleared, then shot Tony a grin. "All right, Tone?"

"Yeah, fine." Tony grinned back. He wasn't

bothered by the blizzard. Living here in the depths of the country, he'd got used to severe winter weather. Anyway, he loved going out with Dad on breakdown jobs whenever he got the chance. Dad liked having him along, too. As he said, Tony was getting to the age where he could be useful, and in a one-man business that was sometimes an answer to his prayers.

The wipers whined and the engine rumbled as they drove slowly and carefully along the road. Visibility was awful: the headlights hardly seemed to penetrate the murk, and the snow whirling towards the screen looked like a mad kaleidoscope. Tony was half hypnotized by it – until, suddenly and shockingly, a bulky, dark shape loomed to one side of the road.

"Dad, look out!" Tony shouted. At the same instant the shape lurched out of the hedge towards them. If they hadn't been going so slowly they would have crashed into it. As it was, the thing barrelled across their path, shapeless and unrecognizable in the dark and whirling snow. For one moment Tony saw – or thought he did – two glowing red dots, like devilish eyes glaring at him. Then they winked out, and the object vanished through the hedge on the other side.

Dad stopped the truck and they both sat

gasping and staring. Tony's heart was pounding with shock. Then Dad let out a long whistle.

"Phew – that was close!" he said.

"What *was* it?" Tony hissed.

"I've no idea. Much too big to be a person, and too big for a deer, too."

Tony grinned shakily. "Unless it was Rudolph the Red-Nosed Reindeer. Maybe Santa's got lost!"

Dad grinned too, but then his face sobered. "Seriously, it could've been an escaped horse, or even a bull. You'd better phone Oldley Farm. Tell George Foster what we saw, and ask him to alert the other farmers."

"OK." Tony grabbed the mobile. George Foster was puzzled; as far as he knew no one had lost any livestock, but he promised to ring round just in case.

As Tony hung up again, a road sign showed dimly in the headlights. "T-junction," said Dad. "This is it. Look out for the oak tree."

Tony saw it a few seconds later, a gaunt, bare silhouette in the murk. The truck slowed to a crawl and Dad wound down the window, peering out.

"There's something under the tree, but I can't make out what it is. And there's no sign of the bloke..."

"Hang on," said Tony. "There – look."

A figure moved near the tree trunk. In fact it looked as if he'd been hiding behind it, and only peered out when he saw the truck stopping. Dad shouted, "Hello? We're Belton's Breakdowns!" and the figure scrambled out of a small snowdrift and came scuttling towards them. He was a small, fat man, and he seemed to have snow all over his head.

The truck halted and Tony and Dad jumped down into the whirling snow. The man stumbled up to them – and it took all the self-control Tony possessed not to burst out laughing. Because the guy was wearing a Santa outfit. He had the whole rig; red coat and trousers, black boots with white fur tops, even the white hair and beard (which Tony had thought were snow). And to cap it all, red cheeks and an extremely red nose.

But if he looked like Santa, he didn't act like him. Instead of a jolly "Ho, ho, ho!" he snarled, "Took you long enough, didn't it? Thought you were supposed to be local!"

"We got here as quickly as we could," Dad said calmly. "You can't drive fast in these conditions, if you want to get where you're going."

The man scowled at the clear hint that this

was exactly what he'd been doing. "Keeping me hanging around in this lot – anything could have happened!" He flung a strangely nervous glance over his shoulder, and Tony noticed with surprise that, despite the bitter cold, he was sweating.

"Well, go on then, get it sorted!" he growled, waving in the general direction of the tree. "I'm late enough already!"

Dad raised his eyebrows at Tony, but he didn't say anything. They trudged towards the tree, leaving the man huddling by the truck. As they approached, Tony thought he heard an odd noise on the other side of the hedge – a sort of shuffling... Remembering what they'd glimpsed on the road, he paused, listening. But all he could hear now was the wind, so he shrugged and trudged on.

Then he forgot the strange noise, as he saw what the man had been travelling in.

It was a sleigh. A whopping great Santa Claus-style sleigh, loaded with brightly wrapped parcels. Tony clapped a hand over his mouth to stop himself from laughing aloud, as he realized what must have happened.

This guy was Santa, all right! He must be the same Santa who'd been in town this morning, when Tony went in with Mum for some last-minute shopping. He'd been sitting in his sleigh, waving at all the kids while a tape deck played syrupy Christmas music. The idea was that you paid a quid for some tacky "present" worth about 2p, and the money was supposed to go to an Old Reindeer's Home or something. Santa (Tony decided at that moment that the guy was going to be "Santa" from now on) had finished his stint, the sleigh had been put on a lorry, and at the junction it had come off. The lorry driver must have trundled on completely oblivious, and Santa had been left stranded. This was *brilliant.* In fact it was just about the funniest thing going!

Dad thought so, too. One look at the sleigh and he guffawed loudly.

"What are you laughing at?" Santa shouted. "There's nothing funny about this, I can tell you! If that thing—"

"Sorry!" Dad's laughter subsided and he started examining the sleigh with a torch in his hand. After a couple of minutes, he went back to the truck with Tony at his heels.

"It doesn't look too badly damaged," Dad told Santa. "How did – " A snort of laughter, which he disguised as a cough – "how did it happen?"

Santa turned purple. "How do you *think* it happened?" he snapped. "It went completely out of control! I hit the tree, the traces broke, and it ran away!"

"He didn't come back for you, then? Didn't realize what had happened?"

"Of course it realized! Blasted animal! If it wasn't for the fact that it's on hire, I'd – I'd – " He was turning purple again, and the sentence collapsed in a splutter.

"Animal?" Dad repeated, baffled. "I was talking about the driver."

"What driver? *I'm* the driver! You think I'm going to waste even more money hiring a blasted driver as well as a blasted reindeer that isn't even a *proper* blasted reindeer?" Santa snarled. "I'll give them 'The Creatures Agency: Your Wish Is Our Command'!" His face twisted and he mimicked savagely, " 'Sorry, Mr Claus, but it's the only one we've got left. All the others are booked – it *is* Christmas you, know.' Of course I know it's blasted Christmas! Who *would* know better than me? Eh? *Eh?*"

He glared almost accusingly at Tony as he said this, but before Tony could think of a reply (which probably wouldn't have been anything better than "Er...") Dad cut in.

"Hang on, let me get this straight. Are you telling me that a *reindeer* was pulling this thing?"

"Of course it was!" Santa exploded. "What did you think was pulling it, a team of mice?"

Dad scratched his head in disbelief. "A reindeer?"

"Yes, yes, YES! That's what I said, didn't I?"

"It wasn't on a low-loader?"

"Low-loader?" Santa screeched. "What the dickens would I be doing with a blasted low-loader? Started making flying ones, have they?" He made a grab for his pocket, fished out a flat bottle and took a huge swig. Tony, fascinated, watched his Adam's apple bobbing as the drink went down. Then Dad nudged him and jerked his head towards the sleigh. Tony nodded, understanding, and Dad said, "Right, sir. We'll just take another look, then we'll see what we can do."

They left Santa muttering under his breath and walked over to the sleigh again. When they were out of earshot, Dad said, "He's drunk. All that rubbish about reindeer – he's probably been boozing since lunchtime!"

Tony hunched further into his coat as a ferocious gust whipped the snow around them. "I reckon he's the same guy who was in the market square today. I thought then he looked a bit ... you know." He waggled a hand.

"Right. He's probably having delusions. Disgusting, getting into that state! He ought to be sacked."

154

"I expect he will be, anyway. I mean, there's nothing for Santa to do once Christmas Day comes, is there?" Tony pointed out. He felt sort of sorry for the guy, however grumpy and difficult he might be.

Dad relented a bit. "Well, I suppose we can't leave him to stew in his own juice, much as I'd like to. As you say, it *is* Christmas… Right, then. The first thing's to see if it's possible to hitch this contraption to the truck. Then, if we can, we'd better find out where he wants it taken."

It took them several minutes to work out that the truck could transport the sleigh, and when Dad was satisfied he cleared his throat and called to Santa.

"Er-hem! All right, Mr, er…"

"Claus!" Santa barked indignantly.

Dad rolled his eyes in one of those *give-me-strength* looks. "Mr Claus, of course. Whatever really did happen, we'd better get your vehicle back to base, so we can get a proper look at the damage and see if it can be fixed."

"Base?" said Santa. "Where's that?"

"My yard. It's only small, but I've got—"

"Is there a proper phone there?"

"Well, yes—"

"That'll do, then! Anywhere with a proper phone – blasted mobiles are useless over any

155

distance. Right, right, right – get on with it, then." He peered into the dark; nervously again, Tony thought. "And hurry up!"

Tony could hear Dad's teeth clenching. "Stand clear," he said curtly. "I'll back the truck up, while Tony sorts out the fixing points on the sleigh."

Santa came scurrying to where Tony was, and stood very close to him. He still kept peering into the snowfall, and, curious, Tony peered, too. But there wasn't anything there.

Or was there? Because, just for a split second, Tony thought he saw something a short way off: two glowing red sparks. He blinked, and when he looked again, the sparks had gone. Tony shook his head. He was imagining things. Or maybe the red points had been the rear lights of a car in the distance, and the snow gave the illusion that they were much closer than they really were.

He'd forgotten about the mysterious shape on the road.

As he bent to examine the sleigh, Santa suddenly, unexpectedly, nudged him in the ribs.

"Oof!" Tony jumped and banged his head on the side of the sleigh. Santa didn't apologize. Instead, he said, "Your dad."

"What about him?" Tony rubbed his head, annoyed.

"He doesn't believe it, does he?"

"Doesn't believe what? 'Scuse me." Tony nudged him aside.

"That I'm Santa Claus."

"Course he doesn't." There was a strong smell of booze on the guy's breath, Tony noticed now. Dad had been right. "And neither do I."

A peculiar growling sound came from the man's throat. "But I *am*!"

Tony was losing patience. "Yeah, sure," he said. "And I'm the fairy on top of the Christmas tree. Look, if you want to do something useful, tell me where we can fix the chains to this thing."

The truck's engine started up at that moment and the roar drowned out Santa's reply. Revving, the truck began to reverse slowly closer – and Tony jumped a second time as a hand suddenly clamped on his shoulder.

"Look," Santa hissed in his ear, breathing fumes. "Your dad's a grown-up, right? They don't understand. But you're young enough to have some sense left. So if I ask you a question, will you give me a straight answer?"

Tony shook his hand off. "I don't know what you're on about," he said over the truck's noise.

157

"Move out of the way, will you? You're holding everything up – I thought you were in a hurry!"

"Oh, I am. And so would you be, if you knew what I know!"

"Yeah, sure," said Tony exasperatedly. "But I don't know what you know, do I?"

"Answer my question, and you just might!"

He wasn't going to give up, Tony realized. The only way this job would get done was to let him say his bit then shut up.

He sighed. "All right. What's the question, then?"

Santa looked quickly, almost furtively, behind him. "On your way here ... did you *see* anything?"

Tony's face was blank. "Like what?"

"Like anything that shouldn't have been there. Anything unusual, or ... *weird*."

An image came into Tony's brain, and he frowned. "Well ... since you ask..."

"Yes? Yes?" Santa started to fidget excitedly from one foot to the other. "Tell me!"

A funny little squirming feeling was making Tony's stomach uncomfortable. "There *was* something... It came out of the hedge, right in front of us. We nearly hit it, but Dad managed to stop in time."

"What was it?"

"I ... don't really know. It disappeared before we could get a proper look. A big animal of some kind; maybe a horse. Or a bull."

"Oh, hell's bells!" said Santa.

Tony's eyes narrowed. "Do you know something about it?"

Santa hauled the bottle out of his pocket and took a swig that was much bigger than the previous one. He finished, wiped his mouth, shoved the bottle back again, and said, "Yep."

A connection clicked, and Tony stared at Santa in astonishment. "You're not trying to say it was – your reindeer?"

"*My* reindeer?" said Santa. "Ha. *Ha!*" Out came the bottle again. "I wish! But no; blasted Rudolph had to go and get blasted flu, didn't he? Laid up in his stable, too weak to do anything except droop around feeling sorry for himself! So what do I get? A hire job. That turns out to be totally insane, deranged and *dangerous!*"

He took yet another swig and started to pace to and fro, his boots kicking up flurries of snow. Tony's gaze followed him. He didn't know what to say. Obviously the guy wasn't just drunk but barking mad into the bargain. Should he humour him? Or should he just tell him to shut up, stop pratting around and leave him and Dad to get on with their work?

He was still dithering when Santa turned on his heel and marched right up to him.

"Listen, boy," he said, pushing his face so close to Tony's that Tony could see the red veins on his nose, "I'll tell you now: what you saw was *not* a horse or a bull. It was the *thing* that was pulling my sleigh. Now it's on the loose. And if it isn't found and dealt with pretty soon, there's going to be *trouble*. Do you understand?"

Tony opened his mouth to say no, he actually hadn't the foggiest what the guy was talking about, but a renewed roar from the truck drowned his voice. Dad had manoeuvred it into the right position; the engine gave a final deafening rev, then settled to a lumpy tickover, and Dad jumped down from the cab.

"Right. All set," he said. "Tony, you and Mr – er – get in the cab. No point standing around in the snow if you don't have to. I'll fix the chains."

Santa didn't need telling twice. He hared back to the truck and was scrambling in before Tony could even move. Dad watched him disparagingly, then said, "I'm going to charge him double for this job," and stomped off towards the sleigh. Tony stared at the cab, where Santa was now making himself comfortable. Barking mad? It had to be the answer, didn't it?

Yet something was making him uneasy.

Something in the guy's voice when he'd been telling his far-fetched story. The old man believed it. He genuinely did. And he was *scared*.

And now, Tony *had* remembered the strange shape on the road. The glaring red eyes.

A bull? None of the local farmers seemed to have lost one.

So could it have been something else...?

Feeling very uncomfortable suddenly, he hurried to the truck and climbed into the cab. There was a pool of melting snow on the seat, making it soggy. And Santa was fiddling with Dad's mobile.

Tony forgot his unease. "Hey!" he said indignantly. "What are you doing? That's ours!"

Santa jabbed buttons, then snarled and shook the mobile violently. "And it's no better than mine! Useless blasted things!"

Tony grabbed the mobile back before he could throw it out of the window. "Leave it alone, then!" he snapped.

"Oh, sure!" said Santa. "Just leave it and everything'll be all right, is that it? Well, it won't be all right! That thing's *out* there, and it's *mean!*" His beard jerked up and down, as though he was struggling to bite back some extremely rude words. Then he fixed Tony with a piercing blue stare. "I know what you're thinking; oh, yes I do. You're thinking: he's just a barmy old boozer who's having delusions. Well, you'd better think again!"

"Oh, come on!" Tony protested. "What d'you expect anyone to think? All that stuff about Rudolph getting flu, and you having to hire something, and..." He spread his hands helplessly. "It's crazy!"

"It is. But not in the way you're thinking." Santa craned out of the window and looked nervously around. He'd started to sweat again. "I hope your dad hurries up. I want to get out of here fast, in case that brute's still hanging about!" He pushed his face up close to Tony's. "Look, I'll tell you the whole lot, and if you still scoff at it, that's your problem. No one can say I didn't warn you!"

"Warn me...?" Tony's unease started to creep back. "What about?"

"Just *listen*!" growled Santa. "Right. So Rudolph gets flu, which means I've got to find something else to pull my sleigh. So I get on to the Agency, and they tell me all the reindeer are booked—"

"You said all that before," Tony interrupted.

"All *right*! I don't know; kids are so impatient these days! Not like the old times when—"

162

"What about the reindeer?"

Santa glared at him, but got back to the subject. "So I say, I've got to have something, and they say, OK, we'll see what we can do. Ten minutes later I get a call; it's sorted. So I go out to start getting my sleigh loaded, and there it is. *Ha!*" He reached for his bottle again and Tony said, "Haven't you had enough?"

"Oh, I've had enough, all right!" He glugged down some more. Strangely, though he must have guzzled his way through most of the bottle, it still appeared to be full...

"I don't know what they made that thing from," he continued ominously. "Oh, it *looked* like a reindeer. They're clever, these agencies. But I reckon they'd put together half a troll, half a dragon and half a werewolf!" That made three halves, but arithmetic didn't seem to be Santa's strong point. "One look at those red eyes glaring at me, and I thought: Santa, old mate, this thing's going to be trouble!"

Tony thought: *Red eyes...?* But before he could think any more, there was a sudden clank of chains from outside. Santa jumped as if he'd sat on a red-hot cushion, then slapped a hand to his heart. "Don't *do* that to me!" he snarled.

Tony looked out of the window. "Dad's hurrying up, like you wanted," he said. "You'd better get on with the story before he comes back."

"Still don't believe me, do you?"

Tony didn't answer, and Santa made a noise that was half sigh and half growl. "Suit yourself. Well, anyway, it was pretty obvious that the best way to keep the thing under control was make sure it had plenty to eat. So I call the Agency back, don't I? What sort of food should I give it? Oh, anything, they said. Horses, cows, sheep, elephants, killer whales – it isn't fussy. Fine, I say, but what's its *favourite*? Know what they replied?"

"Pterodactyls?" Tony suggested, straight-faced. This story was getting so ludicrous that he was forgetting his creepy feelings, and had decided that the thing on the road was a horse or bull after all. He relaxed. But Santa didn't.

"Ha, ha," he said sarcastically. "Pterodactyls are extinct even where I come from. No, sonny. That thing's favourite food is *people*. And it's *specially* fond of nice, juicy *kids*!"

As he said the word "kids", Santa gave a big, significant nod, as if he expected Tony to open his eyes very wide and gasp, "Oh, how horrible, I believe you now, I really do!" Tony didn't do any such thing. He only stared, blankly, pityingly, and at last said, "You really *are* nuts!"

For a second or two Santa stared back at him. Then out came the bottle all over again, and he took the most enormous gulp yet.

"Right!" he said when he'd finished. "That is *it*. I've told you, I've warned you, and no one can say I haven't! If you take no notice, then that's your funeral. Possibly quite literally!"

"Yeah, yeah." Tony started to heave himself off the seat. "I've had enough of all this. I'm going to help Dad finish, then we'll get you back to the yard."

Santa made a grab for his arm, but missed. "Look," he said, sounding almost desperate, "I don't *want* anyone to be eaten by this thing! But don't you *see*; I had to have something to pull the sleigh, or no one would've got any presents tonight! I thought I could control it! But it ate five sheep and a couple of pigs, and it was *still* hungry, and then it bit the ends of the reins off and I couldn't slow the sleigh down, and—"

The rest of the ramble disappeared into thin air. Tony had gone.

"Dad." He trudged up to the sleigh and jerked a thumb over his shoulder. "That guy's completely out of his tree. Let's get rid of him as quick as we can!"

Dad grinned sympathetically. "OK. It's just about ready now. You go and—"

He stopped as, from somewhere in the distance, came a peculiar, thrumming roar.

"*Pfphftt!*" The sound was Santa spluttering; clearly he'd been having another guzzle. Then his quavering voice floated from the cab. "Wh-what was *that?*"

Dad shrugged. "Dunno. Lorry, probably, but it's a long way off. Sounds like he might have some wheelspin."

Santa bawled, "What?" and Tony reluctantly went over to the cab.

"Stop flapping! It's only a lorry somewhere."

"It didn't sound like a lorry to me! It sounded like – like *it!*" The distant roar came again, and Santa flinched, his eyes growing as round and bulgy as ping-pong balls. "Oh, no!" he whispered.

Dad called back, "That driver's having trouble! Right, then: chains are all fixed, so let's get her hoisted up and moving!"

In five more minutes, they were off. Santa had stopped trying to talk to anyone. He huddled down in the seat, nursing his bottle and muttering into his beard. Every so often Tony caught a word or two: things like "Oh, no..." and "It can't, it can't..." He ignored it. And he ignored the squirmy, uneasy sensation in his stomach, which still wouldn't *quite* go away. He was tired, that was all. Getting a bit hungry, too. Never mind; they'd soon be home. And what a story they had to tell Mum!

With the sleigh dangling and swaying precariously in the chains Dad had fastened, they rumbled slowly through the treacherous lanes towards home. Tony had the feeling that, though he stayed hunched down, Santa was furtively watching and listening very hard. But there were no more distant roaring noises, and no dark shapes loomed out of the hedge. Once, he did glimpse twin red glows again. But he was certain, now, that it was only a distant car.

At last the lights of the house came in sight. Dad turned into the yard, and as he switched the truck's engine off, the back door opened and Mum came out.

"Everything all right?" she called.

Santa peered at her, as if to make sure that she wasn't some kind of monster. Then he hissed to Tony, "Where's the phone? The proper one?"

"In the house," said Tony. "But you'd better ask—"

Too late. Santa was already out of the cab and scurrying towards the door. He whizzed past an astonished Mum and disappeared inside.

"It's all right, Mum," Tony said, following. "We'll explain in a minute."

He could see Santa in the hall, dialling frenziedly. "Hello, hello? Creatures Agency? You know who this is, and you know why I'm calling! I don't care if you're closed for Christmas now; you blasted well *listen*! Yes, it did! Clean away, and now it's out there somewhere! ... What? ... Well, what do you *think* I want you to do? I want you to find it and get it back, that's what! Before we've got a major mess on our hands!"

Mum looked at Tony, mystified. "Whatever's he on about?"

Tony shrugged helplessly. Santa finished off his conversation with some colourful threats about what he'd do if things weren't sorted, then slammed the receiver down, picked it up again and dialled another number.

"Archibald? It's me. Look, there's been a bit of an accident. The sleigh ... yes, it did... No idea, but that's the agency's problem... Look, get a team of the lads together, will you, and come down here to collect me? No, I didn't finish ... have to use the spare one, and Rudolph'll just have to do it, even if he still feels like last night's leftovers... Well, bad luck! Don't ask, just *tell* him! Right. Right. See you in a bit."

Bang went the receiver again. Santa sighed

gustily and his shoulders relaxed as he turned round.

"Madam." He addressed Mum with pompous dignity, and actually bowed to her. "Thank you for your kind hospitality. And now, if you'll excuse me..."

Mum goggled as he marched past her to the door. On the step, he met Dad coming in.

"Right, Mr – er," Dad said briskly. "The sleigh'll be fine where it is until we can get it moved to wherever it's supposed to go. Now, we'd better see about getting you some transport home."

Santa bowed to Dad, too. Tony wished he had a camera handy to record the look on Dad's face. "Thank you," he said, all dignified again, "but that's all been taken care of. My own people are coming to fetch me, and they'll deal with the sleigh as well. So it only remains for me to wish you good night!"

Mum and Dad didn't notice it, but Tony saw that Santa was having a very hard time hanging on to his self-control. He wanted out of here and he wanted out fast, and all this bowing and politeness was a complete sham. He *was* scared. He really, truly was.

Dad looked baffled but relieved. "Oh, well," he said. "If you're sure..." He fished for the invoice pad he carried in his top pocket. "OK then; I'll write out the bill."

"Bill? Oh – oh yes, of course." Santa waited while Dad scribbled, then looked at the piece of paper. "Yes ... no problem there. The – um – stuff I'll need's in the sleigh, so I'll just fetch it and sort that out."

He scurried back outside, looking right and left as he went. Tony and his parents waited.

And waited.

And waited.

"It doesn't take *this* long to get a chequebook, does it?" said Mum at last.

Dad was gulping a well-earned cup of tea and hadn't noticed the minutes passing. Frowning, he got up and went outside. Tony followed, and found him standing in the yard with his fists on his hips and a look of baffled outrage on his face.

"He's gone!" Dad said explosively, taking in the yard with a sweep of one hand.

"And – and so's the sleigh!" Tony didn't believe it! How could anyone have shifted that thundering great object, without any noise and in the space of a few minutes? It simply wasn't possible!

But where the sleigh had stood was just an empty space in the yard.

Dad was opening and shutting his mouth like a stranded fish, and he finally spluttered, "They must have crept in and taken it!"

"Who must?" said Tony.

"These 'people' of his, whoever they are. And he went with them! Did a runner, without paying!"

"Wait a minute." Tony pointed through the snow. "What's that, over there?"

Something was lying on the ground where the sleigh had been. It wasn't very big, and it looked angular and lumpy, a bit like a sack of coal.

It *was* a sack. But it wasn't full of coal.

It was full of festively wrapped parcels.

"What the—" Dad stared down at the sack in amazement.

"Looks like Christmas presents," said Tony in a small voice.

There was a note pinned to the sack. Still standing out in the snow, they read it by torchlight. It said:

GRATEFUL THANKS. SPLENDID JOB.
MERRY CHRISTMAS.
LOVE, SANTA.
P.S. HO, HO, HO.

Dad's mouth worked open and shut again. But Tony had seen something else: another scrap of paper, tucked in among the parcels. It had his name on it.

He pushed the paper into his pocket before Dad noticed it, and they lugged the sack indoors. Mum was hopping up and down demanding an explanation, but Tony knew that they weren't going to explain even a tenth of this. Leaving Dad to make a start, he retreated to the hall, and unfolded his note.

It was in the same writing as the Merry Christmas one. But the message was very different.

"Dear Tony," it said. *"I heard what I heard, and I know what I know. You used to believe in Santa, so for old times' sake do him a favour tonight. Lock all your doors and windows. And leave a fire burning, so nothing can get down the chimney. They'll sort it, eventually. But it might take a while. And after you've helped me, it'd be a pity if* **you** *were its dinner. Bye, now. See you next year. S.C."*

Tony read the note three times. The squirmy feeling was back, and his legs didn't feel too steady.

Then he remembered the phone. Who *had* Santa been calling?

He picked up the receiver and hit the redial button, carefully watching the phone's digital readout screen. 0-0-0-0-0- (*Uh?* Tony thought. *That's not a proper number!*) 0-0-0-1.

That was it. And at the other end, a bell was ringing...

He held his breath. *Click* went the line. And a voice started to speak. It was muffled, and the line was very crackly, so he could only make out a few words.

"...*closed for Christmas. There is no answering service, so* ... (crackle, splutter) ... *our apologies. Thank you for calling. Goodbye.*"

And without him doing a thing, the line cut itself off.

The number had gone from the digital readout, and Tony couldn't remember how many noughts there'd been. Eight? Nine? He shook his head. Probably better not to ask. He had a funny feeling that he wasn't supposed to know that number. Nobody was supposed to. Ever.

In the kitchen, Mum was loudly bombarding Dad with questions, and Dad was struggling to get a word in edgeways. Better go to the rescue, Tony thought. He started towards the door...

Outside, there was a peculiar noise.

It wasn't quite a growl and it wasn't quite a roar, but it was pretty close to both. Tony went to the front door, grasped the latch, hesitated. Should he look? Or would it be better to pretend to himself that nothing had happened...?

He couldn't resist. He opened the door a crack, and peered out into the night.

At first he thought there was nothing there. Then, in the dark, a big, bulky shadow moved. Slowly, stealthily. He heard a *huff*, like something breathing. Something very large and unpleasant. And he thought he saw, just for one moment, two glimmering red embers that *might* have been eyes...

Tony shut the door again, very quietly. He locked it. He bolted it. He put the chain on. In the kitchen, his parents' voices were getting louder. Tony didn't go in to join them. Instead, he tiptoed to the sitting-room, then upstairs. He'd just go round and see that all the windows were locked. And he'd put some more coal on the fire. Quite a lot more.

The guy had been barking mad, of course. No possible doubt of that.

But it didn't hurt, did it, to make *absolutely* sure...?

Creepy Creatures
by Lorna Read

Creepy Creatures

Words & Music by Lorna Read

I think I'd bet - ter warn you, you're going to get a fright! There's
Hair - y, sca - ry crea - tures, you'll meet them an - y - where. They
Spook - y, tooth - y Crea - tures are nev - er what they seem. We

some - thing in the cor - ner when you turn out the light. It's slith - er - y and
lurk be - hind your teach - er or un - der - neath your chair. They're wait - ing round the
know they're out to reach us 'cos that's their lit - tle scheme. We hope they'll nev - er

slob - ber - ry and soon it's going to bite! Fea - thered or hair - y, ev - er so scar - y
co - rn - er, - face them if you dare! Fea - thered or hair - y, ev - er so scar - y,
get - us, we pray it's just a dream. Fea - thered or hair - y, ev - er so scar - y,

Crea - tures in the night. **CHORUS:** Fright - ful, bite - ful, spite - ful when they're
Creat - ures ev - er - y - where.
Creat - ures make us SCREAM!

scorned. Sneak - y Cre - a - tures, cree - py Cre - a - tures, you've been warned!

Last time: Sneak - y Cre - a - tures, cree - py Cre - a - tures, YOU'VE BEEN WARNED!

Are they ordinary animals – or are they **Creatures**?

To find out about other **Creatures** titles by **Louise Cooper** turn the page and read on

Creatures

Once I Caught
a Fish Alive

"It *is* bigger," Gemma said uneasily. "In fact, I'd say it's grown about three centimetres since yesterday."

Paul didn't answer. He dared not, because he agreed with her and didn't want to acknowledge it. The fish gazed back through the glass and fanned its tail and fins lazily. They had both been trying to outstare it, but had found they couldn't; the fish had a patience and determination that was unnerving, and it simply wouldn't look away. Paul thought: *It's challenging us. It knows we're getting the wind up, and it's enjoying every moment. What sort of creature have I landed myself with?*

Creatures

If You Go Down
to the Woods

"It's gone!" Caroly whispered. Her face was dead white and she looked as if she was going to be sick. "But how? It can't have *walked*!"

"Can't it?" said Alex. The horrible thought she had had earlier was creeping back. The owl. The fox. The bag. All those tracks in the snow.

And Chaz. . .

"They're coming alive," she said in a small, fearful voice. "The animals in our props and costume bits . . . They're *all* coming alive!"

Creatures

See How They Run

He spun round. Behind him, on the floor, were six very large rats. They were sitting up on their haunches, front paws raised, staring at him.

Then he saw eight more in the doorway. These were smaller – more like normal size – but they were sitting up, too. Very still. Very quiet. *Staring.*

Jon swallowed. He moved the torch – and there were more rats, on a fallen beam that lay at a sloping angle between the ceiling and the floor. Lined in a row, sitting up, and absolutely motionless as they watched with their mean, beady little eyes.

The ugly truth dawned on Jon even before he started to swing the torch around in a wide arc. There were rats everywhere.

Creatures

Who's Been Sitting in My Chair?

"Opal!" Not knowing whether to feel relieved or annoyed, Rhoda started towards the armchair.

Then suddenly, in the cushioned depths of the chair's seat, a pair of eyes appeared.

There was nothing else. No face, no shape; just *eyes*. They were almond-shaped, amber-yellow, and had huge black pupils that glared furiously at Rhoda.

The purring stopped. There was an instant's absolute silence – then a piercing animal screech ripped through the room, an appalling din that battered Rhoda's ears. Her mouth opened in the beginnings of a terrified scream—

Creatures

Atishoo! Atishoo! All Fall Down!

Turning away from the cage, Kel started to walk towards the door. The others followed.

And Chocky said, quite clearly, "Susie won't hurt *you*."

They all stopped dead. Turned. Stared. Birds can't grin, but if Chocky had been human there would have been a smirk on his face.

"Susie won't hurt *you*," he repeated, then paused as if he was thinking – or listening to something no one else could hear. "Susie *likes* you."

Creatures

Give a Dog a Bone

Chris bit his lip, then his shoulders heaved. "OK. But it sounds totally stupid. There's Nathaniel's statue, right? And Lancer's next to him. Well, I could see them both clearly from my window."

He hesitated again, then with an effort turned to face Pippa. He looked embarrassed. And he also looked frightened.

"I wasn't dreaming," he said, "and I didn't imagine it. The moon was out and the statues had shadows. The statue of Lancer was completely still; I mean, it's made of stone, so of course it was. But . . ." He swallowed. "Honest, Pippa, I'm not joking. Lancer's shadow was *moving*."